MW00571913

Collectanea Hermetica Volume I

Sub Lux,

Darcy Küntz

# ARCANVM HERMETICÆ PHILOSOPHIÆ OPVS.

In quo occulta Naturæ & Artis circa Lapidis Philoſophorum materiam & operandi modum canonicè & ordinatè fiunt manifeſta.

*Opus einſdem authoris* ANONYMI.

PENES NOS VNDA TAGI.

PARISIIS,
Apud NICOLAVM BVON, ſub ſigno D. Claudij, & Hominis Syluestris.
MDC. XXIII.

*Cum priuilegio Regis.*

Separate title page for *Hermetic Arcanum* (1623).

# COLLECTANEA HERMETICA

EDITED BY


W. WYNN WESTCOTT, M.B., D.P.H.

*(Supreme Magus of the Rosicrucian Society.*
*Master of the Quatuor Coronati Lodge.)*


---

VOLUME I.

---

AN ENGLISH TRANSLATION OF THE

## HERMETIC ARCANUM

OF

## PENES NOS UNDA TAGI.

## 1623

WITH A PREFACE AND NOTES BY

"SAPERE AUDE", FRA. R.R. ET A.C.


**2011**
**GOLDEN DAWN RESEARCH TRUST**

# Collectanea Hermetica
# Volume I: Hermetic Arcanum



•∘∘○◯○∘∘•

ISBN: 978-1-9269820-0-7.

First published as Volume I of the *Collectanea Hermetica* by Theosophical Publishing Society, 1893.

Revised and Corrected Edition.
First Printing, 2011.

**GOLDEN DAWN RESEARCH TRUST**
P.O. Box 15964 Austin, Texas 78761-5964 USA

## Contents

## Illustrations

# GENERAL PREFACE

TO THE

# "COLLECTANEA HERMETICA."

---

When William Wynn Westcott established the Hermetic Order of the Golden Dawn in 1888 he realised a substantial part of his great dream: to breathe new life into the Western Mystery Tradition and to disseminate its content throughout the English-speaking world. The rituals of Westcott's Order enabled its initiates to experience the practical expression of this Tradition through what was implicit in the ceremonies themselves and to learn the basic elements of its spiritual philosophy from the instructional texts that supplemented the rituals. But members of the Golden Dawn were not expected to remain at such a basic level: they were required to rise above it by studying the works of the great adepts of the past. It did not seem to Westcott to be an unreasonable requirement; were not such works readily at hand in the great library of the British Museum? They were, but usually as single copies so that only one member at a time, of those who lived in or near London, could obtain access to them. How then could the lengthening queue of local members and the large body of those who lived in Yorkshire, Edinburgh, the West Country and elsewhere in Britain be supplied with their necessary texts?

Most of the major primary works of the Western Mystery Tradition were old, long out-of-print and rare; few of them existed in English translation and booksellers bemoaned the scarcity of 'Works on Occult Philosophy'. J.H. Slater, himself to become a prominent member of the Golden Dawn, referred to this scarcity in his *Library Manual* of 1883:

> "The booksellers, if asked, will say that they cannot procure these works in sufficient quantities, and that whenever they are offered for sale they are immediately bought up at extravagant prices."

Of course, among the significant number of articulate and cultured men and women who were members of the Golden Dawn there were some who paid these prices—Woodman and Westcott spring immediately to mind—and there were a number of fine libraries assembled by occultists of the Victorian era, but collectors, even if they are also *adepti*, are notoriously unwilling to lend their treasures to others. They could, however, be persuaded to let their books be used for the preparation of new editions, and in this way Westcott found the solution to his problem.

There was already one specialist-publishing house, that of George Redway, that published new titles on Western occultism and occasionally issued reprints of classics from the past. Thus, members of the Golden Dawn could read historical and critical studies of Alchemy, Kabbalah and the Rosicrucians, and could absorb the wisdom of Eliphas Levi in English, but the speculative works and translations of Anna Kingsford were printed in limited editions and soon disappeared. As did Redway and many of his titles with him, for in 1889 his firm was merged with the larger publishing concern of Kegan Paul and it would be seven years before he returned to his specialist field as an independent publisher. In his place came the Theosophical Publishing Society, which set up at the Adelphi, in London, in the Summer of 1888, but it was weighted towards Buddhism, Hinduism and 'Theosophy'—all as understood by Madame Blavatsky—until Westcott made use of his friendship with her to undermine, slowly and subtly, this heavy Eastern bias. His influence appeared first in Blavatsky's *Theosophical Glossary*, and after her death in the willingness of her successors to invest in the wisdom of both the Graeco-Roman world and in the Western Mysteries as a whole.

So it was that in 1893 the first volume of Westcott's remarkable series *Collectanea Hermetica* made its appearance. And it was very much his series, for all save one of the eight volumes were edited by Westcott, either wholly or partly, by name or motto and two were partially translated by him. Only three other members, Florence Farr, Percy Bullock and Frank Coleman, contributed to the series, of which Florence Farr was the most significant: the final volume, *Egyptian Magic* (1896), being an original work of her own. Westcott, however, had the last word. In 1902, he added a supplementary volume to the series, a new edition of his earlier work on *Numbers*, just as he had preceded it in 1893 with a revision of his translation of the *Sepher Yetzirah*. Both of these titles were in an identical format to that of the series, and in the same blue cloth.

But did the series serve its purpose? Ostensibly, it was published to provide important texts of Western occultism to a discerning public at a reasonable price, while it also served the private interests of members of the Golden Dawn by supplying them with what were, in effect, textbooks on many of the Order's major areas of study: Alchemy, the Kabbalah, Gnosticism, the Mystery Religions and Egyptian traditions. The introductions and notes were the work of competent and knowledgeable members of the Order who, while anonymous to the world at large, were easily identified by their fellow adepts from their mottos. And the members made full use of them. For example, we know from the Second Order diary that Yeats regularly worked with the alchemical texts, while surviving copies of titles that belonged to the Revd. A.H.E. Lee are all heavily annotated by him. What is perhaps surprising is who among the members did not contribute to *Collectanea Hermetica*. Dr. Woodman had died before they began to appear and A.E. Waite was busy with his own publishing concern, but why is there nothing by Mathers? He could have written with ease, and with apparent if not real knowledge, on the Kabbalah, on magic or on divination, but his absence is very noticeable.

Of course, by 1893 there was already a breach between Mathers and Westcott that widened over the next seven years. Mathers was following his own, increasingly eccentric path down the darker byways of magic and it is unlikely that the Theosophists would have welcomed his work, even if Westcott had sought it. Perhaps we should be relieved that he did not, for as it stands the series still offers the reader a clear and deep insight into the mind-set of the occultists and would-be magicians of the late Victorian era. What else each title offers is explained by the new generation of scholarly enthusiasts who have enriched the series with their own perceptions of the texts and studies that so fascinated the original members of the Hermetic Order of the Golden Dawn.

Robert A. Gilbert,
*Tickenham, North Somerset,*
March 2011.

# PREFACE

TO THE

# "COLLECTANEA HERMETICA."

---

HERMETIC students find very great difficulty in securing copies of the old Rosicrucian tracts and other notable volumes of occult lore, and I have been urged by many earnest members of the Rosicrucian Society to undertake the Editorship of a series of small volumes, which are to provide some of the texts of the greatest value in Hermetic research. Among my personal friends and fellow-students are many who have made a long study of the Occult Sciences, of the Kabbalah, of Alchemy, and of the Higher Magic, and these have assured me of their support in this undertaking. The Notes which are added to each volume are partly taken from mediæval commentators, and are partly those of my coadjutors. The Societas Rosicruciana, as an Institution, is not answerable for the opinions expressed; all responsibility falling upon the actual writers.

The Notes are intended to assist those who have made some progress in the study of Hermetic Philosophy; to the casual reader they may be as incomprehensible as the text itself, and where the general reader finds a simple definite statement such is probably a *Reveiling* and not a *Revelation*.

W. W. W.

# INTRODUCTION

TO THE

# "HERMETIC ARCANUM."

IT is quite an honour to be asked to write an introduction to this first volume of the *Collectanea Hermetica*. The complete series of books is really one of those foundational sources that lay at the heart of Western occultism, and the Hermetic Tradition in particular.

I remember the first time I was able to examine several of the original volumes a friend had collected. It was in the early 1970s when I visited his basement "alchemist lair". There amid flasks, retorts, and crucibles he was anxious to show me his latest find, the first three volumes of the *Collectanea Hermetica*.

We poured over them for several hours before our heads were saturated. These were books I never dreamed I would be able to study, much less be able to afford. We mused how one day the computer technology, which was very limited, would allow us to access rare books from around the world. That time has since come to pass and I think I have collected more texts electronically than were in the Great Library of Alexandria. Of course, the majority of alchemists I have met are true bibliophiles and the thought of seriously pursuing an alchemical text from a computer screen seems just unnatural.

Hermetic and alchemical writings cannot be read as you would a novel; they need to be savoured slowly, contemplated, cross-referenced, and digested. Nothing can replace an actual book in hand for such work and study. I am very pleased to see this become a possibility through the publication of the *Collectanea Hermetica* series, and making the revised editions available to serious students of the Art.

For over forty years, I have studied the Hermetic Arts both in the library and the laboratory. Like many Western practitioners, I have obtained a strong foundation through the study and practice of materials derived from the teachings of the Golden Dawn and its august body of members. Because I am of a practical nature and a natural born chemist, I gravitated toward the practice of laboratory alchemy, which has laboured under a dark cloud since the High Middle Ages.

The popular interpretation of the alchemical legacy is a psychological one that was developed from the pioneering work of Carl Jung. The psychological interpretation works well with alchemy because the old masters agree that the universe is a mental construct following definite rules. Yet this extends much further than most realize. These same rules or universal laws stretch down from mental and spiritual conditions and even into our physical environment. The study of one will shed light on the other in a true Hermetic relationship of "as above, so below". In the alchemist's laboratory, we can see how nature operates with our own hands and eyes, and we can test theories to see if they hold true.

The most fundamental precept of Hermetic Philosophy teaches us that everything we perceive, both visible and invisible, is derived from a single source. Through a series of steps, the One becomes the many. This series of steps or operations of Nature were studied by the ancient alchemists, and the written books were presented to students through archetypal imagery and myth.

In reading an alchemical text, it is not unusual to run into a dragon, a unicorn, or even a strangely coloured lion. Chemical terms cannot always be taken at face value either, especially when dealing with the alchemist's "*Tri Prima*" or three essentials of Salt, Sulphur, and Mercury, which have multiple levels of meaning. At the ultimate level, these correspond to the essential qualities of the divine source: omniscience, omnipotence, and omnipresence. At another level, it is the interplay between intelligence, energy, and matter. At the physical level, these same qualities can take on the properties of volatile essences, oily waxy resinous materials, and crystalline alkali salts.

The practice of laboratory alchemy is currently experiencing a global revival. Apart from the ever-elusive gold making thing, the potential for new types of medicinal agents is unlimited. Some of the ancient alchemical preparations are being reproduced and undergoing clinical trials right now. This is especially true for metallic medicines prepared according to Indian and Arabic alchemical sages. These Eastern works can actually shed quite a bit of light on parts of the current text of the *Hermetic Arcanum*.

There is a world-view in alchemy that life and intelligence is contained in every natural organism, even the rocks and minerals. The author Jean d'Espagnet instructs us in "Canon 21" of the *Hermetic Arcanum*, that we should begin our work with those materials that still possess their natural living qualities undamaged by crude industry. If we begin with a dead body we will be just wasting our time, so our goal is to awaken into activity the innate generative power of the materials. Mercury is the medium in which and through the entire process occurs. This is not the common mercury, but as Jean d'Espagnet states, it is "extracted out of it by the philosophers' skill".

Many of the Western alchemical authors tell us that the use of metallic mercury is a "blind" or a trick to the unwary. But is that statement itself a blind? Mercury is the centrepiece of both Chinese and Indian alchemy where it is considered the root of all the metals, hidden under the guise of a red dragon. Metallic mercury is dangerous stuff to be sure, but it is a logical choice since it was the only material known in ancient times that could reliably turn gold into a liquid state. Moreover, in the East, natural mercury was considered to be adulterated by various accidents of

Nature and by man handling it (compare "Canon 50"). Through processes of purification and sublimation, these accidental imbalances are removed and the mercury is no longer considered to be common. Although currently illegal to import in many countries, these medicines derived from alchemically processed metallic mercury called *Rasa Medicines*, are still being used with success in modern India against a wide variety of diseases. One of these Rasa Medicines, called *Makaradhvaja*, is held to possess healing and life-extending properties, which is not far from a similar description in the *Hermetic Arcanum*. It is prepared by amalgamating specially purified metallic mercury with gold and then sublimating that amalgam with prepared mineral sulphur. The end product of the Makaradhvaja is a red crystalline powder. Many of the Canons contained in the present text, both theoretical and practical, can be applied to its preparation. Once the theory is understood, variations of the material and processes are possible.

One of the most popular formula variations in Western alchemy is the use of the mineral Stibnite as the source of the metallic or philosophers' mercury through whose agency the leaven (gold or silver) is awakened into activity. Stibnite, often described as a black scaled dragon, is the sulphide ore of the metal Antimony. The use of Antimony was held to introduce the necessary generative force more abundantly and thus shorten the time required to produce the Stone. Its association with alchemical works extends into the remote past. Stibnite is refined into the coveted "Star Regulus", a metallic form of Antimony, which is believed to contain a fiery quality that can be harnessed to ignite the leaven to multiply. Antimony, itself the subject of many alchemical tracts, is a treasure trove of medicine currently unrecognized and awaiting rediscovery by modern pioneers of the Sacred Science of laboratory alchemy.

These medicines do not operate according to normal medical practices as Dr. Theodor Kerkring states in his 1723 commentary on Basil Valentine's *Triumphal Chariot of Antimony*:

"These Medicaments, which perform their Operations, not by sensible force, as Cathartics, Emetics, Diaphoretics, and the like are wont to operate, but insensibly uniting their own more pure Universal Spirit unto our Spirits, amend Nature and restore it to health."

I have always sided with Paracelsus who taught that laboratory alchemy should focus on the preparation of powerful medicines for health of the body and spiritual advancement, but the lure of gold through the agency of the Philosophers' Stone has captured the hearts and minds of many throughout the centuries. Counterfeit gold and silver have fooled many, but the ancients knew full well how to differentiate the real from the fool's article. They used a process of fire assaying, which consisted of using molten lead to analyse the gold and silver content in the material. This process has been in use for at least 4000 years. Jean d'Espagnet mentions it as a test of the final product calling it the "trial by fire", and the ability to resist the searching Saturn (see "Canon 33").

The possibility of metallic transmutation, though difficult to attain, has been claimed to be a true phenomenon in both the Eastern and Western alchemical traditions. Even the genius, Sir Isaac Newton, believed this was possible and that he himself was very close to solving this alchemical riddle. By the 1800s, the chemical elements were viewed as being immutable building blocks, and their transmutation was an impossibility. Alchemy was severely taken to task for attempting to transmute the chemical elements and it was considered "debunked". At the dawn of the 20th century, the world again was becoming open to new ideas impart due to the discovery of radioactivity, and that the natural transmutation of elements upset the rigid mechanical view of science.

Recent advances in catalytic reactions, nuclear chemistry, and quantum physics have placed the promises of the alchemist back on the playing field. Cold fusion and other low-energy nuclear transformations are receiving global interest and the possibility of a material such as the Philosophers' Stone seems less of a *chimera* than it has in the last 200 years.

The Hermetic Philosophy as a whole is a very uplifting and life-affirming world view, but the road of the alchemist is an arduous one. It is referred to as the Great Work, and there are no shortcuts. The old masters of the Art admonish us to "read, re-read, and read again, pray and work" if we are to be successful. Then there will come a day where reason and intuition are equal partners and a whole new world and lifestyle will emerge from within. At the end of the day, alchemy is not about the gold, but about the true nature of reality and ourselves. It is a Sacred Science.

Laboratory alchemy has certainly seen its share of turmoil and scandal throughout the centuries. Based partly on fear, misinterpretation, and outright deceit, it would be a very difficult problem for alchemy to get a fair trial in our modern day. Steeped in magic and mystery, the mere mention of it in "scientific" circles usually evokes the obligatory backward eye roll and judgmental smirk from those with no real knowledge of the matter other than a cloudy historical perspective. It is not primitive chemistry, but part of a profound philosophical view of reality that modern science is only now catching up to. Vast potential on many fronts are just waiting to be tapped into for the benefit of mankind. The magic of yesterday tends to become the science of tomorrow, and we should all leave a little room for magic in our lives.

And so by way of introduction, it is my sincere hope that these volumes of the *Collectanea Hermetica* will help to reopen doors of investigation that have become rusted shut through neglect. Now is the time to savour these volumes as they were meant to be.

Robert Allen Bartlett,
April 2011.

# PREFACE

TO THE

# "HERMETIC ARCANUM."

THE *Arcanum Hermeticum* has been chosen for the first volume of the *Collectanea Hermetica*, because since its first publication in 1623, in the Latin language, no alchymic tract has been more widely read, and no other has been so often reprinted, alike in Latin, German, French and English.

The author, Jean d'Espagnet, was sometime President of the Parliament of Bordeaux, he flourished from 1600 to 1630, and obtained a great reputation as an Hermetic philosopher and alchymist. Two of his alchymic works are alone extant; *Enchiridion Physicæ Restitutæ*, and *Arcanum Philosophilæ Hermeticæ*; of these, the former treats of those theories of chemical constitution upon which the possibility of Transmutation of Metals depends, and the latter of the Practice of Alchymy. The *Arcanum* was first published in 1623 in France; five subsequent French editions in the original Latin are known, and an edition in the French tongue was printed in 1651 from the translation of Jean Bachon. Several editions were also published at Geneva, Kiel, Lubeck, Tubingen and Leipzig. The works of Espagnet are also included in Manget's *Bibliotheca Chemica Curiosa* and in the *Bibliotheca Chemica* of Albineus.

Jean d'Espagnet followed the usual Rosicrucian custom of using a motto instead of his name when publishing Hermetic books. The *Hermetic Arcanum* is signed "Penes nos unda

Tagi;" he also at times added the motto, "Spes mea in Agno est." These mottoes are anagrams. Each contains the letters of "Espagnet," and the two taken together contain also the letters of "Deus (IHVH with the Shin interposed) omnia in nos," but there are two letters over, "A S." The French biographer says, in error, that only one letter, an "E"—his initial—remains over.

Espagnet was not only an Alchymist, but a Mystic as well; he contributed a preface and a sonnet to a work by Pierre de Lancre, entitled *Tableau de l'inconstance des mauvaises Anges*, 1612. He is also notable as having taken a leading part in the prosecution of persons who were supposed to be black magicians, living in the district called Les Landes and among the Pyrenees; but this action appears to have been the result of his position in the Parliament of Bordeaux.

He ornamented the façade of his house in the Rue de Bahutiers, at Bordeaux, with allegorical sculptures and devices; the house has been destroyed, but these ornaments are still to be seen preserved in the gardens of the mayoral residence.

As a natural philosopher, Jean d'Espagnet declined to be led by the notions of Aristotle, and preferred those of the Alexandrian schools. He postulated the ideal of one material universal basis, or *hyle*, from which all varieties of matter have been evolved by stages of development, a necessary doctrine for one who taught the mutual convertibility of the so-called chemical elementary substances. He also insisted upon the importance of representing all manifestation as separable into three worlds, elementary, celestial, and archetypal; this division is related to the scheme of the Four Worlds of the Kabbalists, by a concentration which is recognized by such philosophers. He taught the origin of created things from the chaos of the first matter, which under the energetic impulse of the Divine Force, proceeds from stage to stage of development into heterogeneity. He recognized three stages of matter, the subtle, the mean, and the gross: analogous to the airy, moist, and earthy natures of the Hermetists. Upon these bases his *Enchiridion* is almost a text-book of Rosicrucian Philosophy.

The *Arcanum* describes at considerable length, and with obvious good faith, the procedure of one school of Alchymists in the search for the secret of the Stone Philosophical, and it formulates the stages of the work so that he or she who can read may run. Yet it must be confessed that he has well succeeded in reveiling, as well as revealing, the secret of what was meant by the Prima Materia and the real nature alike of *The* Sulphur, *The* Salt, and *The* Mercury.

Such a work as the *Arcanum*, written by one who knows, is not sent to print, to teach the *public*, to show a cheap and easy way to wealth and luxury, or to assist coiners of spurious moneys, but is intended as a treasure house in which those who have devoted life and love to the quest may find stored up the data and experiences of such as have trodden the Path and have borne tribulation and persecution, counting all loss to be gain in their progress to success and to the possession of that Stone of the Wise, which when obtained can indeed transmute the things of the material world, but does also equally work upon all higher planes, and enables an Adept to soar unheeding into worlds of joy, wisdom, and exultation, which are unseen, unknown, and inconceivable to ordinary mortals, who have chosen the alternative of physical contentment and material happiness.

The original Latin title is given at the first page, together with an English translation.

The German edition of 1685, Leipzig, was entitled: *Das geheime Werck der Hermetischen Philosophie, von Joannes d'Espagnet. Anagr-e-in u. mut. Penes nos unda Tagi.* This has an additional preface, and cap. 138 is numbered 137. "Joannes" must be taken as "Joannus."

An English translation was made by James Hasolle, Esquire, Qui est Mercuriophilus Anglicus [in *Fasciculus Chemicus, or Chymical Collections*]; this is the anagram and pseudonym of Elias Ashmole, famous as an antiquary. Copies of his third edition of 1650 are not uncommon. The present editor of the *Hermetic Arcanum* had at first intended to reprint Ashmole's version in its entirety, but a comparison with the original Latin has induced him to make a revision of Ashmole's translation, because he discovered many important inaccuracies, and also because in some places the language was more forcible and plain than our present delicate manners would appreciate.

S.A. is responsible for most of the Notes; a few are from Sigismund Bacstrom, Frater R.R. et A.C., and others are from the marginal references of an anonymous Adept writing in 1710.

"SAPERE AUDE"
[W. Wynn Westcott]

## TO THE STUDENTS IN,

## AND WELL AFFECTED UNTO

# "HERMETIC PHILOSOPHY,"

*health and prosperity.*†

---

AMONGST the heights of hidden Philosophy, the production of the Hermetic Stone hath of a long time been strongly believed to be the chiefest, and nearest a Miracle, both for the Labyrinths and multitudes of operations, out of which the mind of man, unless it be illuminated by a beam of Divine light, is not able to unwind herself; as also because of its most noble end which promiseth a constant plenty of health and fortunes, the two main pillars of a happy life. Besides, the chief Promoters of this Science have made it most remote from the knowledge of the vulgar sort by their Tropes and dark expressions, and have placed it on high, as a Tower impregnable for Rocks and Situation, whereunto there can be no access unless God direct the way. The study of hiding this Art hath drawn a reproach upon the Art itself and its Professors: for when those unfortunate Plunderers of the Golden Fleece by reason of their unskillfulness felt themselves, beat down from their vain attempt, and far unequal unto such eminent persons; they in a furious rapture at desperation, like mad-men, waxed hot against their fame and the renown of the Science, utterly denying anything to be above their cognizance and the sphere of their wit, but what was foolish and frothy: And because they set upon a business of damage to themselves, they have not ceased to accuse the chief Masters of hidden Philosophy of falsehood.

Nature of impotency, and Art of cheat not for any other reason, then that they rashly condemn what they know not, nor is this condemnation a sufficient revenge, without the addition of madness to snarl and bite the innocent with infamous slanders. I grieve (in truth) for their hard fortune, who whilest they reprove others, give occasion of their own conviction, although they justly suffer a hellish fury within them. They moil and sweat to batter the obscure principles of the most hidden Philosophy with troops of arguments, and to pull up the secret foundations thereof with their devised engines: which yet are only manifest by the skillful, and those that are much versed in so sublime Philosophy, but hid from strangers: Nor do these quick-sighted Censors observe, that whilst they malign another's credit, they willingly betray their own. Let them consider with themselves, whether they understand those things which they carp at; What Author of eminency hath divulged the secret elements of this Science, the Labyrinths and windings of operations, and lastly, the whole proceedings thereof?

What *Oedipus* hath sincerely and truly explained unto him the figures and entangled dark speeches of Authors? With what Oracle, what Sibyll, have they been led into the Sanctuary of this Holy Science? In fine, how were all things in it made so manifest, that no part remains yet unveiled? I suppose they will not otherwise answer my question, when thus, that they have pierced all things by the subtlety of their wits; or confess that they were taught (or rather seduced) by some wandering Quack or Mountebank, who hath crept into a good esteem with them, by his feigned countenance of a Philosopher. O wickedness! who can silently suffer these Palmer-worms to gnaw upon the same labour, and glory of the wise? Who can with patience hear blind men, as out on a Tripod judging of the Sun? But it is greater glory to contemn the hurt less darts of babblers, then to repel them. Let them only disdain the treasure of Nature and Art, who cannot obtain it. Nor is it my purpose to plead the doubtful cause of an unfortunate Science, and being condemned, to take it into tuition: Our guiltless Philosophy is no whit criminal: and standing firm by the aid of eminentest Authors and fortified with the manifold experience of divers ages, it remains safe enough from the fopperies of prattlers, and the snarlings of envy. However Charity hath incited me, and the multitude of wanderers induced me, taking pity on them, to present my light, that so they may escape the hazard of the night: by help whereof they may not only live out, but also procure an enlargement both to their Life and fading Fortunes.

This small Treatise penned for your use (ye Students of Hermetic Philosophy) I present unto you, that it may be dedicated to those, for whose sake it was written. If any perhaps shall complain of me, and summon me to appear as guilty of breach of silence for divulging secrets in an itching style, ye have one guilty of too much respectfulness towards you, confessing his fault, sentence him if you please; so that my crime may supply the place of a reward to you: The offence will not be displeasing unto you, and the punishment (I doubt not) pleasant unto me, if I shall find myself to have erred in this only, hereby you may put an end to erring for the future.

"PENES NOS UNDA TAGI"
[Jean d'Espagnet]

Note:

†. Reprinted from the *Arcanum, or Great Secret of Hermetic Philosophy*, and published in *Fasciculus Chemicus, or Chymical Collections*. Translated by James Hasolle [Elias Ashmole], 1650. The Text has been modernized to match Westcott's translation.–D.K.

ARCANUM:

OR,

The grand Secret

OF

HERMETICK

PHILOSOPHY.

WHEREIN,

The Secrets of NATURE and ART, concerning the Matter and Manner of making the Philosophers Compoſition, are orderly and methodically manifeſted.

*The Work of a concealed Author.*

Penes nos unda Tagi.

The third Edition amended and *enlarged.*

Separate title page for *Hermetic Arcanum* (1650).

# Arcanum Hermeticæ Philosophiæ Opus.

IN QUO OCCULTA NATURÆ ET ARTIS CIRCA LAPIDIS PHILOSOPHORUM MATERIAM ET OPERANDI MODUM CANONICE ET ORDINATE FIUNT MANIFESTA.

*Opus authoris anonymi,*

**PENES NOS UNDA TAGI.**

M DC XXIII.

---

# THE SECRET WORK

OF THE

# HERMETIC PHILOSOPHY

WHEREIN THE SECRETS OF NATURE AND ART CONCERNING THE MATTER OF THE PHILOSOPHERS' STONE AND THE MANNER OF WORKING ARE EXPLAINED IN AN AUTHENTIC AND ORDERLY MANNER.

*The Work of an Anonymous Author,*

**PENES NOS UNDA TAGI.**

---

EDITED BY "SAPERE AUDE."

# 2

# The Hermetic Arcanum.

## CANON I.

THE beginning of this Divine Science is the fear of the Lord[1] and its end is charity and love toward our Neighbour; the all-satisfying Golden Crop is properly devoted to the rearing and endowing of temples and hospices; for whatsoever the Almighty freely bestoweth on us, we should properly offer again to him. So also Countries grievously oppressed may be set free; prisoners unduly held captive may be released, and souls almost starved may be relieved.

2. The light of this knowledge is the gift of God, which by His will He bestoweth upon whom He pleaseth. Let none therefore set himself to the study hereof, until having cleared and purified his heart,[2] he devote himself wholly unto God, and be emptied of all affection and desire unto the impure things of this world.

3. The Science of producing Nature's grand Secret, is a perfect knowledge of universal Nature and of Art concerning the Realm of Metals; the Practice thereof is conversant with finding the principles of Metals by Analysis, and after they have been made much more perfect to conjoin them otherwise than they have been before, that from thence may result a catholic Medicine, most powerful to perfect imperfect Metals, and for restoring sick and decayed bodies, of any sort soever.

4. Those that hold public Honours and Offices or be always busied with private and necessary occupations, let them not strive to attain unto the acmé of this Philosophy; for it requireth the whole man,[3] and being found, it possesseth him, and he being possessed, it debarreth him from all other long and serious employments, for he will esteem other things as strange, and of no value unto him.

5. Let him that is desirous of this Knowledge, clear his mind from all evil passions, especially pride,[4] which is an abomination to Heaven, and is as the gate of Hell; let him be frequent in prayer[5] and charitable;[6] have little to do with the world;[7] abstain from company keeping; enjoy constant tranquillity;[8] that the Mind may be able to reason more freely in private and be highly lifted up;[9] for unless it be kindled with a beam of Divine Light, it will not be able to penetrate these hidden mysteries of Truth.

6. The *Alchymists* who have given their minds to their well-nigh innumerable Sublimations, Distillations, Solutions, Congelations, to manifold Extraction of Spirits and Tinctures, and other Operations more subtle than profitable, and so have distracted themselves by a variety of errors, as so many tormentors, will never be inclined again by their own Genius to the plain way of Nature and light of Truth; from whence their industrious subtlety hath twined them, and by twinnings and turnings, as by the Lybian Quicksands, hath drowned their entangled Wits: the only hope of safety for them remaineth in finding out a faithful Guide[10] and Master,[11] who may make the Sun clear and conspicuous unto them and free their eyes from darkness.

7. A studious *Tyro* of a quick wit, constant mind, inflamed with the study of Philosophy, very skilful in natural Philosophy, of a pure heart, complete in manners, mightily devoted to God, though ignorant of practical Chymistry, may with confidence enter into the highway of Nature and peruse the Books of the

best Philosophers; let him seek out an ingenious and sedulous Companion for himself, and not despair of obtaining his desire.

8. Let a Student of these secrets carefully beware of reading or keeping company with false Philosophers;[12] for nothing is more dangerous to a learner of any Science, than the company of an unskilled or deceitful man by whom erroneous principles are stamped as true, whereby a simple and credulous mind is seasoned with false Doctrine.

9. Let a Lover of truth make use of few Authors, but of the best note and experienced truth; let him suspect things that are quickly understood, especially in Mystical Names and Secret Operations;[13] for truth lies hid in obscurity; for Philosophers never write more deceitfully—than when plainly, nor ever more truly—than when obscurely.

10. As for the Authors of chiefest note, who have discoursed both acutely and truly of the secrets of Nature and hidden Philosophy, Hermes and Morienus Romanus amongst the Ancients are in my judgment of the highest esteem; amongst the Moderns, Count Trevisan, and Raimundus Lullius are in greatest reverence with me; for what that most acute Doctor hath omitted, none almost hath spoken; let a student therefore peruse his works, yea let him often read over his Former Testament, and Codicil, and accept them as a Legacy of very great worth. To these two volumes let him add both his volumes of Practice, out of which Works all things desirable may be collected, especially the truth of the First Matter, of the degrees of Fire, and the Regimen of the Whole, wherein the final Work is finished, and those things which our Ancestors so carefully laboured to keep secret. The occult causes of things, and the secret motions of nature, are demonstrated nowhere more clearly and faithfully. Concerning the first and mystical Water of the Philosophers he hath set down few things, yet very pithily.

11. As for that Clear Water sought for by many, found by so few, yet obvious and profitable unto all, which is the Basis of the Philosophers' Work, a noble Pole, not more famous for his learning than subtlety of wit, who wrote anonymously, but whose name notwithstanding a double Anagram hath betrayed,[14] hath in his *Novum Lumen Chymicum*, *Parabola* and *Ænigma*, as also in his Tract on *Sulphure*, spoken largely and freely enough; yea he hath expressed all things concerning it so plainly, that nothing can be more satisfactory to him that desireth knowledge.

12. Philosophers do usually express themselves more pithily in types and enigmatical figures (as by a mute kind of speech) than by words; see for example, Senior's Table, the Allegorical Pictures of *Rosarius*, the Pictures of Abraham Judaeus in Flamel, and the drawings of Flamel himself;[15] of the later sort, the rare Emblems of the most learned Michael Maiërus wherein the mysteries of the Ancients are so fully opened, and as new Perspectives they present antiquated truth, and though designed remote from our age yet are near unto our eyes, and are perfectly to be perceived by us.

13. Whosoever affirmeth that the Philosophers' grand Secret is beyond the powers of Nature and Art, he is blind because he ignores the forces of Sol and Luna.

14. As for the matter of their hidden Stone, Philosophers have written diversely; so that very many disagreeing in Words, do nevertheless very well agree in the Thing; nor doth their different speech argue the science ambiguous or false, since the same thing may be expressed with many tongues, by divers expressions, and by a different character, and also one and many things may be spoken of after diverse manners.

15. Let the studious Reader have a care of the manifold significations of words, for by deceitful windings, and doubtful, yea contrary speeches (as it should seem), Philosophers wrote

their mysteries, with a desire of veiling and hiding, yet not of sophisticating or destroying the truth; and though their writings abound with ambiguous and equivocal words; yet about none do they more contend than in hiding their Golden Branch:–

— Quem tegit omnis
Lucus; et obscuris claudant convallibus umbræ.[16]

Which all the groves with shadows overcast,
And gloomy valleys hide.

Nor yieldeth it to any Force, but readily and willingly will follow him, who:–

Maternas agnoscit aves,
— et geminæ cui fortè Columbæ
Ipsa sub ora viri crelo venêre volantes.[17]

Knows Dame *Venus* Birds —
And him to whom of Doves a lucky pair
Sent from above shall hover 'bout his Ear.

16. Whosoever seeketh the Art of perfecting and multiplying imperfect Metals, beyond the nature of Metals, goes in error, for from Metals the Metals are to be derived; even as from Man, Mankind; and from an Ox only, is that species to be obtained.

17. Metals, we must confess, cannot be multiplied by the instinct and labour of Nature only; yet we may affirm that the multiplying virtue is hid in their depths, and manifested itself by the help of Art: In this Work, Nature standeth in need of the aid of Art; and both do make a perfect whole.

18. Perfect Bodies as Sol and Luna are endued with a perfect seed; and therefore under the hard crust of the perfect Metals the Perfect Seed lies hid; and he that knows how to take it out by the Philosophers' Solution, hath entered upon the royal highway; for:–

— In auro
Semina sunt auri, quamvis abstrusa recedant
Longius.[18]

In Gold the seeds of Gold do lie,
Though buried in Obscurity.

19. Most Philosophers have affirmed that their Kingly Work is wholly composed of Sol and Luna; others have thought good to add Mercury to the Sol; some have chosen Sulphur and Mercury; others have attributed no small part in so great a Work to Salt mingled with the other two. The very same men have professed that this Clear Stone is made of one thing only, sometimes of two, or of three, at other times of four, and of five; and yet though writing so variously upon the same subject, they do nevertheless agree in sense and meaning.

20. Now that (abandoning all blinds) we may write candidly and truly, we hold that this entire Work is perfected by two Bodies only; to wit, by Sol and Luna rightly prepared, for this is the mere generation which is by nature, with the help of Art, wherein the union of male and female doth take place, and from thence an offspring far more noble than the parents is brought forth.

21. Now those Bodies must be taken, which are of an unspotted and incorrupt virginity;[19] such as have life and spirit in them;[20] not extinct as those that are handled by the vulgar; for who can expect life from dead things; and those are called impure which have suffered combination; those dead and extinct which (by the enforcement of the chief Tyrant of the world)[21] have poured out their soul with their blood by Martyrdom; flee then a fratricide from which the most imminent danger in the whole Work is threatened.

22. Now Sol is Masculine, forasmuch as he sendeth forth active and energizing seed; Luna is Feminine or Negative and she is called the Matrix [and vessel] of Nature, because she receiveth the sperm [of the male in her womb], and fostereth

it by monthly provision, yet doth Luna not altogether want in positive or active virtue.[22]

23. By the name of Luna Philosophers understand not the vulgar Moon, which also may be positive in its operation, and in combining acts [is] a positive part. Let none therefore presume to try the unnatural combination of two positives, neither let him conceive any hope of issue from such association; but he shall join Gabritius to Beia,[23] and offer sister to brother in firm union, that from thence he may receive Sol's noble Son.

24. They that hold Sulphur and Mercury to be the First Matter of the Stone, by the name of Sulphur, they understand Sol [and common Luna]; by Mercury the Philosophic Luna; so (without dissimulation) good Lullius[24] adviseth his friend, that he attempt not to work without Mercury and Luna for Silver; nor without Mercury and Sol for Gold.

25. Let none therefore be deceived by adding a third to two: for Love admitteth not a third; and wedlock is terminated in the number of two; love further extended is not matrimony.

26. Nevertheless Spiritual love polluteth not any virgin; Beia might therefore without fault (before her betrothal to Gabritius) have felt spiritual love, to the end that she might thereby be made more cheerful, more pure, and fitter for the union.

27. Procreation is the end of lawful Wedlock. Now that the progeny may be born more vigorous and active, let both the combatants be cleansed from every ill and spot, before they are united in marriage. Let nothing superfluous cleave unto them,[25] because from pure seed comes a purified generation, and so the chaste wedlock of *Sol* and *Luna* shall be finished when they shall enter into combination, and be conjoined, and Luna shall receive a soul from her husband by this union; from this conjunction a most potent King shall arise, whose father will be *Sol* and his mother *Luna*.

28. He that seeks for a physical tincture without Sol and Luna, loseth both his cost and pains: for Sol afforded a most plentiful tincture of redness, and Luna of whiteness, for these two only are called perfect; because they are filled with the substance of purest Sulphur, perfectly clarified by the skill of nature. Let thy Mercury therefore receive a tincture from one or other of these luminaries; for anything must of necessity possess a tincture before it can tinge other bodies.

29. Perfect metals contain in themselves two things, which they are able to communicate to the imperfect metals. Tincture and Power of fixation; for pure metals, because they are dyed and fixed with pure Sulphur, to wit, both white and red, do therefore perfectly tincture and fix, if they be fitly prepared with their proper Sulphur and Arsenic: otherwise they have not strength for multiplying their tincture.

30. Mercury is alone among the imperfect metals, fit only to receive the tincture of Sol and Luna in the work of the Philosophers' Stone, and being itself full of tincture can tinge other metals in abundance; yet ought it (before that) to be full of invisible Sulphur, that it may be the more coloured with the visible tincture of perfect bodies, and so repay with sufficient Usury.

31. Now the whole tribe of Philosophers do much assert and work mightily to extract Tincture out of gold: for they believe that Tincture can be separated from Sol, and being separated increases in virtue but:—

> Spes tandem Agricolas vanis eludit aristis.

> Vain hope, at last the hungry Plough-man cheats
> With empty husks, instead of lusty meats.

For it is impossible that Sol's Tincture can at all be severed from his natural body, since there can be no elementary body made up by nature more perfect than gold, the perfection whereof proceedeth from the strong and inseparable union of pure colouring Sulphur with Mercury; both of them being admirably pre-disposed thereunto by Nature; whose true separation nature denieth unto Art. But if any liquor remaining be extracted (by the violence of fire or waters) from the Sun, it is to be reputed a part of the body made liquid or dissolved by force. For the tincture followeth its body, and is never separated from it. That is a delusion of this Art, which is unknown to many Artificers themselves.

32. Nevertheless it may be granted, that Tincture may be separable from its body, yet (we must confess) it cannot be separated without the corruption of the tincture: as when Artists offer violence to the gold destroying by fire, or use *Aqua fortis* [*i.e.*, Nitric acid in water], thus rather corroding than dissolving. The body therefore if despoiled of its Tincture and Golden Fleece, must needs grow base, and as an unprofitable heap turn to the damage of its Artificer, and the Tincture thus corrupted can only have a weaker operation.

33. Let Alchymists in the next place cast their Tincture into Mercury, or into any other imperfect body, and as strongly conjoin both of them as their Art will permit; yet shall they fail of their hopes in two ways. First, because the Tincture will neither penetrate nor colour beyond Nature's weight and strength; and therefore no gain will accrue from thence to recompense the expense and countervail the loss of the body spoiled, and thus of no value; so:–

Cum labor in damno est, crescit mortalis egestas.

Want is poor mortal's wages, when his toil
Produces only loss of pain and oil.

Lastly, that debased Tincture applied to another body will not give that perfect fixation and permanency required to endure a strong trial, and resist searching Saturn.

34. Let them therefore that are desirous of Alchemy, and have hitherto followed Impostors and Mountebanks, found a

retreat, spare no time nor cost, and give their minds to a work truly Philosophical, lest the *Phrygians* be wise too late, and at length be compelled to cry out with the prophet, "*Strangers have devoured his strength*".[26]

35. In the Philosophers' work more time and toil than cost is expended: for he that hath convenient matter, need be at little expense; besides, those that hunt after great store of money, and place their chief end in wealth, they trust more to their riches, than their own art. Let, therefore, the too credulous Tyro beware of pilfering pick-pockets, for while they promise golden mountains, they lay in wait for gold; they demand bright gold (*viz.*, money beforehand), because they walk in evil and darkness.

36. As those that sail between Scylla and Charybdis[27] are in danger from both sides: unto no less hazard are they subject who pursuing the prize of the Golden Fleece, are carried between the uncertain Rocks of the Sulphur and Mercury of the Philosophers. The more acute students by their constant reading of grave and credible Authors, and by the radiant sunlight, have attained unto the knowledge of Sulphur, but are at a stand at the entrance of their search for the Philosophers' Mercury; for Writers have twisted it with so many windings and meanderings, involved it with so many equivocal names, that it may be sooner met with by the force of the Seeker's intuition, than be found by reason or toil.

37. That Philosophers might the deeper hide their Mercury in darkness, they have made it manifold, and placed their Mercury (yet diversely) in every part and in the forefront of their work, nor will he attain unto a perfect knowledge thereof, who shall be ignorant of any part of the Work.

38. Philosophers have acknowledged their Mercury to be threefold; to wit, after the absolute preparation of the First degree, the Philosophical sublimation, for then they call it "Their Mercury," and "Mercury Sublimated."

39. Again, in the Second preparation, that which by Authors is styled the First (because they omit the First) Sol being now made crude again,[28] and resolved into his first matter, is called the Mercury of such like bodies, or the Philosophers' Mercury; then the matter is called Rebis,[29] Chaos, or the Whole World, wherein are all things necessary to the Work, because that only is sufficient to perfect the Stone.

40. Thirdly, the Philosophers do sometimes call Perfect Elixir and Colouring Medicine—Their Mercury, though improperly; for the name of Mercury doth only properly agree with that which is volatile; besides that which is sublimated in every region of the work, they call Mercury: but Elixir—that which is most fixed cannot have the simple name of Mercury; and therefore they have styled it "Their Mercury" to differentiate it from that which is volatile. A straight way is only laid down for some to find out and discern so many Mercuries of the Philosophers, for those only:—

— Quos aequus amavit
Jupiter, aut ardens evexit ad aethera virtus.[30]

— Whom just and mighty Jove
Advanceth by the strength of love;
Or such who brave heroic fire,
Makes from dull Earth to Heaven aspire.

41. The Elixir is called the Philosophers' Mercury for the likeness and great conformity it hath with Heavenly Mercury; for to this, being devoid of elementary qualities, heaven is believed to be most propitious; and that changeable Proteus[31] puts on and increaseth the genius and nature of other Planets, by reason of opposition, conjunction, and aspect. In like manner this uncertain Elixir worketh, for being restricted to no proper quality, it embraceth the quality and disposition of the thing wherewith it is mixed, and wonderfully multiplieth the virtues and qualities thereof.

42. In the Philosophical sublimation or first preparation of Mercury, Herculean labour must be undergone by the workman; for Jason had in vain attempted his expedition to Colchos without Alcides:–

> Alter in auratam nota de vertice pellem
> Principium velut ostendit, quod sumere possis;
> Alter onus quantum subeas—[32]

> One from on high a Golden Fleece displays
> Which shews the Entrance, another says
> How hard a task you'll find.

For the entrance is warded by horned beasts, which drive away those that approach rashly thereunto, to their great hurt; only the ensigns of Diana and the Doves of Venus[33] are able to assuage their fierceness, if the fates favour the attempt.

43. The Natural quality of Philosophical Earth and the tillage thereof, seems to be touched upon by the poet in this verse:–

> Pingue solum primis ex templo à mensibus anni
> Fortes invertant Tauri —
> — Tunc Zephyro putris se gleba resolvit.[34]

> Let sturdy Oxen when the year begins
> Plough up the fertile soil —
> For Zephyrus then destroys the sodden clods.

44. He that calleth the Philosophers' Luna or their Mercury, the common Mercury, doth wittingly deceive, or is deceived himself; so the writings of Geber teach us, that the Philosophers' Mercury is Argent vive, yet not of the common sort, but extracted out of it by the Philosophers' skill.[35]

45. The Philosophers' Mercury is not Argent vive in its proper nature, nor in its whole substance, but is only the middle and pure substance thereof, which thence hath taken its origin and has been made by it. This opinion of the grand Philosophers is founded on experience.

46. The Philosophers' Mercury hath divers names, sometimes it is called Earth; sometimes Water, when viewed from a diverse aspect; because it naturally ariseth from them both. The earth is subtle, white and sulphurous, in which the elements are fixed and the philosophical gold is sown; the water is the water of life, burning, permanent, most clear, called the water of gold and silver; but this Mercury, because it hath in it Sulphur of its own, which is multiplied by art, deserves to be called the Sulphur of Argent vive. Last of all, the most precious substance is Venus, the ancient Hermaphrodite, glorious in its double sex.

47. This Argent vive is partly natural, partly unnatural; its intrinsic and occult part hath its root in nature, and this cannot be drawn forth unless it be by some precedent cleansing, and industrious sublimation; its extrinsic part is preternatural and accidental. Separate, therefore, the clean from the unclean, the substance from the accidents, and make that which is hid, manifest, by the course of nature; otherwise you make no further progress, for this is the foundation of the whole work and of nature.

48. That dry and most precious liquor doth constitute the radical moisture of metals, wherefore by some of the ancients it is called Glass; for glass is extracted out of the radical moisture closely inherent in ashes which offer resistance, except to the hottest flame; notwithstanding our inmost or central Mercury discovers itself by the most gentle and kindly (though a little more tedious) fire of nature.

49. Some have sought for the latent Philosophical earth by Calcination, others by Sublimation; many among the glass [vessels], and some few between vitriol and salt, even as among their natural vessels; others enjoin you to sublime it out of lime and glass. But we have learned of the Prophet, that "*In the beginning God created the Heaven and the Earth, and the Earth was without form and void, and darkness was upon the face of the Deep, and the spirit of God*

*moved upon the Waters, and God said, Let there be Light, and there was Light; and God saw the Light that it was good, and he divided the light from the darkness*, etc."[36] *Joseph's* blessing spoken of by the same Prophet will be sufficient to a wise man. "*Blessed of the Lord be his Land, for the Apples of Heaven, for the dew, and for the Deep that liveth beneath: for the Apples of fruit both of sun and moon, for the top of the ancient mountains, for the Apples of the everlasting hills*, etc.,"[37] pray the Lord from the bottom of thy heart (my son) that he would bestow upon Thee a portion of this blessed earth.

50. Argent vive is so defiled by original sin,[38] that it floweth with a double infection; the first it hath contracted from the polluted Earth, which hath mixed itself therewith in the generation of Argent vive, and by congelation hath cleaved thereunto; the second borders upon the dropsy and is the corruption of intercutal[39] Water, proceeding from thick and impure water; mixed with the clear, which nature was not able to squeeze out and separate by constriction; but because it is extrinsic, it flies off with a gentle heat. The Mercury's leprosy infesting the body, is not of its root and substance, but accidental, and therefore separable from it; the earthly part is wiped off by a warm wet Bath and the Laver of nature; the watery part is taken away by a dry bath with that gentle fire suitable to generation. And thus by a threefold washing and cleansing the Dragon putteth off his old scales and ugly skin is renewed in beauty.

51. The Philosophical sublimation of Mercury is completed by two processes; namely by removing things superfluous from it, and by introducing things which are wanting. In superfluities are the external accidents, which in the dark sphere of Saturn do make cloudy glittering Jupiter. Separate therefore the leaden colour of Saturn which cometh up out of the water until Jupiter's purple Star[40] smile upon thee. Add hereunto the Sulphur of nature, whose grain and Ferment it hath in itself, so much as sufficeth it; but see that it be sufficient

for other things also. Multiply therefore that invisible Sulphur of the Philosophers until the Virgin's milk come forth: and so the First Gate is opened unto thee.

52. The entrance of the Philosophers' garden is kept by the Hesperian Dragon, which being put aside, a Fountain of the clearest water proceeding from a sevenfold spring floweth forth on every side of the entrance of the garden; wherein make the Dragon drink thrice the magical number of Seven, until having drunk he put off his hideous garments; then may the divine powers of light-bringing Venus and horned Diana, be propitious unto thee.

53. Three kinds of most beautiful flowers are to be sought, and may be found in this Garden of the wise:[41] Damask-coloured Violets, the milk-white Lily, and the purple and immortal flower of love, the Amaranth. Not far from that fountain at the entrance, fresh Violets do first salute thee, which being watered by streams from the great golden river, they put on the most delicate colour of the dark Sapphire; then Sol will give thee a sign. Thou shall not sever such precious flowers from their roots until thou make the Stone; for the fresh ones cropped off have more juice and tincture; and then pick them carefully with a gentle and discreet hand; if the Fates frown not, this will easily follow, and one White flower being plucked, the other Golden one will not be wanting; let the Lily and the Amaranth, succeed with still greater care and longer labour.

54. Philosophers have their sea also, wherein small fishes plump and shining with silver scales are generated; which he that shall entangle, and take by a fine and small net, shall be accounted a most expert fisherman.

55. The Philosophers' Stone is found in the oldest mountains, and flows from everlasting brooks; those mountains are of silver, and the brooks are e'en of gold: from thence gold and silver and all the treasures of Kings are produced.

56. Whosoever is minded to obtain the Philosophers' Stone, let him resolve to take a long peregrination, for it is necessary that he go to see both the Indies, that from thence he may bring the most precious gems and the purest gold.

57. Philosophers extract their stone out of seven stones, the two chief whereof are of a diverse nature and efficacy; the one infuseth invisible Sulphur, the other spiritual Mercury; that one induceth heat and dryness, and this one cold and moisture: thus by their help, the strength of the elements is multiplied in the Stone; the former is found in the Eastern coast, the latter in the Western: both of them have the power of colouring and multiplying, and unless the Stone shall take its first Tincture from them, it will neither colour nor multiply.

58. ℞. [Praxis:] Take the Winged Virgin very well washed and cleansed, impregnated by the spiritual seed of the first male, and fecundated in the permanent glory of her untouched virginity, she will be discovered by her cheeks dyed with a blushing colour; join her to the second [male], [without Jealousy of adultery,] by whose [corporeal] seed she shall conceive again and shall in time bring forth a reverend off-spring of double sex, from whence an immortal Race of most potent Kings shall gloriously arise.

59. Keep up and couple the Eagle and Lion[42] well cleansed in their transparent cloister, the entry door being shut and watched, lest their breath go out, or the air without do privily get in. The Eagle shall snap up and devour the Lion in this combination; afterwards being affected with a long sleep, and a dropsy occasioned by a foul stomach, she shall be changed by a wonderful metamorphosis into a coal black Crow, which shall begin to fly with wings stretched out, and by his flight shall bring down water from the clouds, until being often moistened, he put off his wings of his own accord, and falling down again he be changed into a most White Swan. Those that are ignorant of the causes of things, may wonder with

astonishment when they consider that the world is nothing but a continual Metamorphosis; they may marvel that the seeds of things perfectly digested should end in greatest whiteness. Let the Philosopher imitate Nature in his work.

60. Nature proceedeth thus in making and perfecting her works, that from an inchoate generation it may bring a thing by divers means, as it were by degrees, to the ultimate term of perfection: she therefore attaineth her end by little and little, not by leaps; confining and including her work between two extremes; distinct and severed as by spaces. The practice of Philosophy, which is the imitator of Nature, ought not to decline from the way and example of Nature in its working and direction to find out its happy stone, for whatsoever is without the bounds of Nature is either an error or is near one.

61. The extremes of the Stone are natural Argent vive and perfect Elixir: the middle parts which lie between, by help whereof the work goes on, are of three sorts; for they either belong unto matter, or operations, or demonstrative signs: the whole work is perfected by these extremes and means.

62. The material means of the Stone are of divers kinds, for some are extracted out of others successively: The first are Mercury Philosophically sublimated, and perfect metals, which although they be extreme in the work of nature, yet in the Philosophical work they supply the place of means: of the former the seconds are produced; namely the four elements, which again are circulated and fixed: of the seconds, the third is produced, to wit, Sulphur, the multiplication whereof doth terminate the first work: the fourth and last means are leaven or ointments[43] weighed with the mixture of the things aforesaid, successively produced in the work of the Elixir. By the right ordering of the things aforesaid, the perfect Elixir is finished, which is the last term of the whole work, wherein the Philosophers' Stone resteth as in its centre, the multiplication whereof is nothing else than a short repetition of the previous operations.

63. The operative means (which are also called the Keys of the Work) are four: the first is Solution or Liquefaction; the second is Ablution; the third Reduction; the fourth Fixation. By Liquefaction bodies return into their first form, things concocted are made raw again, and the combination between the position and negative is effected, from whence the Crow is generated: lastly the Stone is divided into four confused elements, which happeneth by the retrogradation of the Luminaries. The Ablution teacheth how to make the Crow white, and to create the Jupiter of Saturn, which is done by the conversion of the Body into Spirit. The Office of Reduction is to restore the soul to the Stone exanimated, and to nourish it with dew and spiritual Milk, until it shall attain unto perfect strength. In both these latter operations the Dragon rageth against himself, and by devouring his tail, doth wholly exhaust himself, and at length is turned into the Stone. Lastly, the operation of the Fixation fixeth both the White and the Red Sulphurs upon their fixed body, by the mediation of the spiritual tincture; it decocteth the Leaven or Ferment by degrees, ripeneth things unripe, and sweeteneth the bitter. In fine, by penetrating and tincturing the flowing Elixir it generateth, perfecteth, and lastly, raiseth it up to the height of sublimity.

64. The Means or demonstrative signs are Colours, successively and orderly affecting the matter and its affections and demonstrative passions, whereof there are three special ones (as critical) to be noted; to these some add a Fourth. The first is black, which is called the Crow's head, because of its extreme blackness, whose crepusculum[44] sheweth the beginning of the action of the fire of nature and solution, and the blackest midnight sheweth the perfection of liquefaction, and confusion of the elements. Then the grain putrefies and is corrupted, that it may be the more apt for generation. The white colour succeedeth the black, wherein is given the

perfection of the first degree, and of the White Sulphur. This is called the blessed stone; this Earth is white and foliated, wherein Philosophers do sow their gold. The third is Orange colour, which is produced in the passage of the white to the red, as the middle, and being mixed of both is as the dawn with his saffron hair, a forerunner of the Sun. The fourth colour is Ruddy and Sanguine, which is extracted from the white fire only. Now because whiteness is easily altered by any other colour before day it quickly faileth of its candour. But the deep redness of the Sun perfecteth the work of Sulphur, which is called the Sperm of the male, the fire of the Stone, the King's Crown, and the Son of Sol, wherein the first labour of the workman resteth.

65. Besides these decretory signs which firmly inhere in the matter, and shew its essential mutations, almost infinite colours appear, and shew themselves in vapours, as the Rainbow in the clouds, which quickly pass away and are expelled by those that succeed, more affecting the air than the earth: the operator must have a gentle care of them, because they are not permanent, and proceed not from the intrinsic disposition of the matter, but from the fire painting and fashioning everything after its pleasure, or casually by heat in slight moisture.

66. Of the strange colours, some appearing out of time, give an ill omen to the work: such as the blackness renewed; for the Crow's young ones having once left their nest are never to be suffered to return. Too hasty Redness; for this once, and in the end only, gives a certain hope of the harvest; if therefore the matter become red too soon it is an argument of the greatest aridity, not without great danger, which can only be averted by Heaven alone forthwith bestowing a shower upon it.

67. The Stone is exalted by successive digestions, as by degrees, and at length attaineth to perfection. Now four Digestions agreeable to the four above said Operations

or Governments do complete the whole work, the author whereof is the fire, which makes the difference between them.

68. The first digestion operateth the solution of the Body, whereby comes the first conjunction of male and female, the commixtion of both seeds, putrefaction, the resolution of the elements into homogeneous water, the eclipse of the Sun and Moon in the head of the Dragon, and lastly it bringeth back the whole World into its ancient Chaos, and dark abyss. This first digestion is as in the stomach, of a melon colour and weak, more fit for corruption than generation.

69. In the second digestion the Spirit of the Lord walketh upon the waters; the light begins to appear, and a separation of waters from the waters occurs; Sol and Luna are renewed; the elements are extracted out of the chaos, that being perfectly mixed in Spirit they may constitute a new world; a new Heaven and new Earth are made; and lastly all bodies become spiritual. The Crow's young ones changing their feathers begin to pass into Doves; the Eagle and Lion embrace one another in an eternal League of amity. And this generation of the World is made by the fiery Spirit descending in the form of Water, and wiping away Original sin; for the Philosophers' Water is Fire, which is moved by the exciting heat of a Bath. But see that the separation of Waters be done in Weight and Measure, lest those things that remain under Heaven be drowned under the Earth, or those things that are snatched up above the Heaven, be too much destitute of aridity.

Hic, sterilem exiguus ne deferat humor arenam,[45]

Here let slight moisture leave a barren Soil.

70. The third digestion of the newly generated Earth drinketh up the dewy Milk, and all the spiritual virtues of the quintessence, and fasteneth the quickening Soul to the body by the Spirit's mediation. Then the Earth layeth up a great Treasure in itself, and is made like the coruscating Moon, afterwards like

to the ruddy Sun; the former is called the Earth of the Moon, the latter the Earth of the Sun; for both of them are begot of the copulation of them both; neither of them any longer feareth the pains of the Fire, because both want all spots; for they have been often cleansed from sin by fire, and have suffered great Martyrdom, until all the Elements are turned downwards.

71. The Fourth digestion consummateth all the Mysteries of the World, and the Earth being turned into most excellent leaven, it leaveneth all imperfect bodies because it hath before passed into the heavenly nature of quintessence. The virtue thereof flowing from the Spirit of the Universe is a present Panacea and universal medicine for all the diseases of all creatures. The digestions of the first work being repeated will open to thee the Philosophers' secret Furnace. Be right in thy works, that thou mayest find God favourable, otherwise the ploughing of the Earth will be in vain; Nor

> Illa seges demum votis respondet avari [46]
> Agricolæ:—

> Will the expected Harvest e'er requite
> The greedy husbandman—

72. The whole Progress of the Philosophers' work is nothing but Solution and Congelation; the Solution of the body, and Congelation of the Spirit; nevertheless there is but one operation of both: the fixed and volatile are perfectly mixed and united in the Spirit, which cannot be done, unless the fixed body be first made soluble and volatile. By reduction is the volatile body fixed into a permanent body, and volatile nature doth at last change into a fixed one, as the fixed nature had before passed into volatile. Now so long as the Natures were confused in the Spirit, that mixed Spirit keeps a middle Nature between Body and Spirit, Fixed and Volatile.

73. The generation of the Stone is made after the pattern of the Creation of the World; for it is necessary, that it have

its Chaos and First matter, wherein the confused Elements do fluctuate, until they be separated by the fiery Spirit; they being separated, the Light Elements are carried upwards, and the heavy ones downwards: the light arising, darkness retreats: the waters are gathered into one place and the dry land appears. At length the two great Luminaries arise, and mineral, vegetable and animal are produced in the Philosophers' Earth.

74. God created Adam out of the mud of the Earth, wherein were inherent the virtues of all the Elements, of the Earth and Water especially, which do more constitute the sensible and corporeal heap: Into this Mass God breathed the breath of Life, and enlivened it with the Sun of the Holy Spirit. He gave Eve for a Wife to Adam, and blessing them he gave unto them a Precept and the Faculty of multiplication. The generation of the Philosophers' Stone, is not unlike the Creation of Adam, for the Mud was made of a terrestrial and ponderous Body dissolved by Water, which deserved the excellent name of *Terra Adamica*, wherein all the virtues and qualities of the Elements are placed. At length the heavenly Soul is infused there into by the medium of the Quintessence and Solar influx, and by the Benediction and Dew of Heaven; the virtue of multiplying *ad infinitum* by the intervening copulation of both sexes is given it.

75. The chief secret of this work consisteth in the manner of working, which is wholly employed about the Elements: for the matter of the Stone passeth from one Nature into another, the Elements are successively extracted, and by turns obtain dominion; everything is agitated by the circles of *humidum* and *siccum*,[47] until all things be turned downwards, and there rest.

76. In the work of the Stone the other Elements are circulated in the figure of Water, for the Earth is resolved into Water, wherein are the rest of the Elements; the Water is Sublimated into Vapour, Vapour retreats into Water, and so

by an unwearied circle, is the Water moved, until it abide fixed downwards; now *that* being fixed, all the elements are fixed. Thus into it they are resolved, by it they are extracted, with it they live and die; the Earth is the Tomb, and last end of all.

77. The order of Nature requireth that every generation begin from *humidum* and *in humidum*. In the Philosophers' work, Nature is to be reduced into order,[48] that so the matter of the Stone which is terrestrial, compact and dry, in the first place may be dissolved and flow into the Element of Water next unto it, and then Saturn will be generated of Sol.

78. The Air succeeds the Water, drawn about by seven circles or revolutions, which is wheeled about with so many circles and reductions, until it be fixed downwards, and Saturn being expelled, Jupiter may receive the Sceptre and Government of the Kingdom, by whose coming the Philosophers' Infant is formed, nourished in the womb, and at length is born; resembling the splendour of Luna in her beautiful and serene countenance.

79. The Fire executes the courses of the Nature of the Elements, extreme Fire assisting it; of the hidden is made the manifest; the Saffron dyeth the Lily; Redness possesseth the cheeks of the blushing Child now made stronger. A Crown is prepared for him against the time of his Reign. This is the consummation of the first work, and the perfect rotation of the Elements, the sign whereof is, when they are all terminated in *Siccum*, and the body void of Spirit lieth down, wanting pulse and motion; and thus all the Elements are finally resolved into Terra.

80. Fire placed in the Stone is Nature's Prince, Sol's Son and Vicar, moving and digesting matter and perfecting all things therein, if it shall attain its liberty, for it lieth weak under a hard bark; procure therefore its freedom that it may succour thee freely; but beware that thou urge it not above measure, for being impatient of tyranny it may become a fugitive, no

hope of return being left unto thee; call it back therefore by courteous words, and keep it prudently.

81. The first mover of Nature is External Fire, the Moderator of Internal Fire, and of the whole Work; Let the Philosopher therefore very well understand the government thereof, and observe its degrees and points; for from thence the welfare or ruin of the work dependeth. Thus Art helpeth Nature, and the Philosopher is the Minister of both.

82. By these two Instruments of Art and Nature, the Stone lifteth itself up from Earth to Heaven with great ingenuity, and slideth from Heaven to Earth, because the Earth is its Nurse, and being carried in the womb of the wind, it receiveth the force of the Superiors and Inferiors.

83. The Circulation of the Elements is performed by a double Wheel, by the greater or extended, and the less or contracted. The Wheel extended fixeth all the Elements of the Earth, and its circle is not finished unless the work of Sulphur be perfected. The revolution of the minor Wheel is terminated by the extraction and preparation of every Element. Now in this Wheel there are three Circles placed, which always and variously move the Matter, by an Erratic and Intricate Motion, and do often (seven times at least) drive about every Element, in order succeeding one another, and so agreeable, that if one shall be wanting the labour of the rest is made void. These Circulations are Nature's Instruments, whereby the Elements are prepared. Let the Philosopher therefore consider the progress of Nature in the Physical Tract,[49] more fully described for this very end.

84. Every Circle hath its proper Motion, for all the Motions of the Circles are conversant about the subject of *Humidum* and *Siccum*, and are so concatenated that they produce the one operation, and one only consent of Nature: two of them are opposite, both in respect of their causes and the effects; for one moveth upwards, drying by heat; another downwards,

moistening by cold; a third carrying the form of rest and sleep by digesting, induceth the cessation of both in greatest moderation.

85. Of the three Circles, the first is Evacuation, the labour of which is in extracting the superfluous *Humidum*, and also in separating the pure, clean and subtle, from the gross and terrestrial dregs. Now the greatest danger is found in the motion of this Circle, because it hath to do with things Spiritual and makes Nature plentiful.

86. Two things are chiefly to be taken heed of in moving this Circle; first, that it be not moved too intensely; the other, that it be not moved for too long a time. Motion accelerated raiseth confusion in the matter, so that the gross, impure and undigested part may fly out together with the pure and subtle, and the Body undissolved be mixed with the Spirit, together with that which is dissolved. With this precipitated motion the Heavenly and Terrestrial Natures are confounded, and the Spirit of the Quintessence, corrupted by the admixture of Earth is made dull and invalid. By too long a motion the Earth is too much evacuated of its Spirit, and is made so languishing, dry and destitute of Spirit, that it cannot easily be restored and recalled to its Temperament. Either error burneth up the Tincture, or turneth it into flight.

87. The Second Circle is Restoration; whose office is to restore strength to the gasping and debilitated body by Potion. The former Circle was the Organ of sweat and labour, but this of restoration and consolation. The action of this is employed in the grinding and mollifying the Earth (Potter-like), that it may be the better mixed.

88. The motion of this Circle must be lighter than that of the former, especially in the beginning of its Revolution, lest the Crow's young ones be drowned in nest by a large flood, and the growing world be drowned by a deluge. This is the Weigher and Assayer of Measures, for it distributeth Water

by Geometrical Precepts. There is usually no greater Secret found in the whole practice of the Work than the firm and justly weighed Motion of this Circle; for it informeth the Philosophers' Infant and inspireth Soul and Life into him.

89. The Laws of this Circle's motions are, that it run about gently: and by little and little, and sparingly let forth itself, lest that by making haste it fall from its measure, and the Fire inherent be overwhelmed with the Waters, the Architect of the Work grow dull, or also be extinguished: that meat and drink be administered by turns, to the end there may be a better Digestion made, and the best temperament of *Humidum* and *Siccum*; for the indissoluble colligation of them both is the End and Scope of the Work. Furthermore see, that you add so much by Watering, as shall be found wanting in assaying, that Restoration may restore so much of the lost strength by corroborating, as Evacuation hath taken away by debilitating.

90. Digestion, the last Circle, acteth with silent and insensible Motion; and therefore it is said by Philosophers, that it is made in a secret furnace; it decocteth the Nutriment received, and converteth it into the Homogeneous parts of the body. Moreover, it is called Putrefaction; because as meat is corrupted in the Stomach before it passeth into Blood and similar parts; so this operation breaketh the Aliment with a concocting and Stomach heat and in a manner makes it to putrefy that it may be the better Fixed, and changed from a Mecurial into a Sulphurous Nature. Again, it is called Inhumation,[50] because by it the Spirit is inhumated, as a dead man buried in the ground. But because it goeth most slowly, it therefore needeth a longer time. The two former Circles do labour especially in dissolving, this in congealing although all of them work in both ways.

91. The Laws of this Circle are, that it be moved by the Feverish and most gentle heat of Dung, lest that the things volatile fly out, and the Spirit be troubled at the time of its

strictest Conjunction with the Body, for then the business is perfected in the greatest tranquillity and ease; therefore we must especially beware lest the Earth be moved by any Winds or Showers. Lastly, as this third Circle may always succeed the second straightways and in due order, as the second [succeeds] the first: so by interrupted works and by course those three erratic Circles do complete one entire circulation, which often reiterated doth at length turn all things into Earth, and makes similarity between opposites.

92. Nature useth Fire, so also doth Art after its example, as an Instrument and Mallet in cutting out its works. In both operations therefore Fire is Master and Perfector. Wherefore the knowledge of Fire is most necessary for a Philosopher, without which as another Ixion (condemned to labour in vain) he shall turn about the Wheel of Nature to no purpose.

93. The name Fire is Equivocal amongst Philosophers; for sometimes it is used by Metonymy for heat; and so there be as many fires as heats. In the Generation of Metals and Vegetables, Nature acknowledgeth a Three-fold Fire; to wit, Celestial, Terrestrial and Innate. The First flows from Sol as its Fountain into the Bosom of the Earth; it stirreth up Fumes, or Mercurial and Sulphurous vapours, of which the Metals are created, and mixeth itself amongst them; it stirreth up that torpid fire which is placed in the seeds of Vegetables, and addeth fresh sparks unto it, as a spur to vegetation. The Second lurketh in the bowels of the Earth, by the Impulse and action whereof the Subterraneous vapours are driven upwards as through pores and pipes, and thrusts outwards from the Centre towards the surface of the Earth, both for the composition of Metals, where the Earth swelleth up, as also for the production of Vegetables, by putrefying their seeds, by softening and preparing them for generation. The third Fire, *viz.*, Innate is also indeed Solar; it is generated of a vapid smoke of Metals, and also being infused with the monthly provision

grows together with the humid matter, and is retained as in a Prison; or more truly, as form is conjoined with the mixed body; it firmly inhereth in the seeds of Vegetables, until being solicited by the point of its Father's rays it be called out, then Motion intrinsically moveth and informeth the matter, and becomes the Moulder and Dispenser of the whole Mixture. In the generation of Animals, Celestial Fire doth insensibly co-operate with the Animal, for it is the first Agent in Nature; for the heat of the female answereth to Terrestrial Fire; when the Seed putrefies, this warmth prepareth it. For truly the Fire is implanted in the Seed; then the Son of Sol disposeth of the matter, and being disposed, he informeth it.

94. Philosophers have observed a three-fold Fire in the matter of their work, Natural, Unnatural, and Contra-Natural. The Natural they call the Fiery Celestial Spirit Innate, kept in the profundity of matter, and most strictly bound unto it, which by the sluggish strength of metal grows dull, until being stirred up and freed by the Philosophers' discretion and external heat, it shall have obtained a faculty of moving its body dissolved, and so it may inform its humid matter, by Unfolding Penetration, Dilatation and Congelation. In every mixed body Natural Fire is the Principle of Heat and Motion. Unnatural Fire they name that which being procured and coming from without is introduced into the matter artificially; that it may increase and multiply the strength of the natural heat. The Fire Contrary to Nature they call that which putrefieth the Compositum, and corrupteth the temperament of Nature. It is imperfect, because being too weak for generation, it is not carried beyond the bounds of corruption: such is the Fire or heat of the menstruum: yet it hath the name improperly of Fire against Nature, because in a manner it is according to Nature, for although it destroys the specific form, and corrupteth the matter, yet it disposeth it for reproduction.

95. It is more credible nevertheless that the corrupting Fire, called Fire against Nature, is not different from the Innate, but the first degree of it, for the order of nature requireth, that Corruption should precede Generation: the fire therefore that is innate, agreeable to the Law of Nature, performeth both, by exciting both successively in the matter: the first of corruption more gentle stirred up by feeble heat to mollify and prepare the body: the other of generation more forcible, moved by a more vehement heat, to animate and fully inform the Elementary body disposed of by the former. A double Motion doth therefore proceed from a double degree of heat of the same fire; neither is it to be accounted a double Fire, for far better may the name of "Fire contrary to Nature" be given to violent and destructive fire.

96. Unnatural Fire is converted into Natural or Innate Fire by successive degrees of Digestion, and increaseth and multiplieth it. Now the whole secret consisteth in the multiplication of Natural Fire, which of itself is not able to Work above its proper strength, nor communicate a perfect Tincture to imperfect Bodies; for although it be sufficient to itself, yet hath it not any further power; but being multiplied by the unnatural, which most aboundeth with the virtue of multiplying, doth act far more powerfully, and reacheth itself beyond the bounds of Nature–colouring strange and imperfect bodies, and perfecting them, because of its plentiful Tincture, and the abstruse Treasure of multiplied Fire.

97. Philosophers call their Water, Fire, because it is most hot, and indued with a Fiery Spirit; again, Water is called Fire by them, because it burneth the bodies of perfect Metals more than common fire doth, for it perfectly dissolveth them, whereas they resist our Fire, and will not suffer themselves to be dissolved by it; for this cause it is also called Burning Water. Now that Fire of Tincture is hid

in the belly of the Water, and manifests itself by a double effect, *viz.*, of the body's Solution and Multiplication.

98. Nature useth a double Fire in the Work of generation, Intrinsic and Extrinsic; the former being placed in the seeds and mixtures of things, is hid in their Centre; and as a principle of Motion and Life doth move and quicken the body. But the latter, Extrinsic, whether it be poured down from Heaven or Earth, raiseth the former, as drowned with sleep, and compels it to action; for the vital sparks implanted in the seeds stand in need of an external motor, that they may be moved and act.

99. It is even so in the Philosophers' work; for the matter of the Stone possesseth his Interior Fire, which is partly Innate, partly also is added by the Philosophers' Art, for those are united and come inward together, because they are homogeneous: the internal standeth in need of the external, which the Philosopher administereth according to the Precepts of Art and Nature; this compelleth the former to move. These Fires are as two Wheels, whereof the hidden one being moved by the visible one, it is moved sooner or later; and thus Art helpeth Nature.

100. The Internal Fire is the middle agent between the Motor and the Matter; whence it is, that as it is moved by that, it moveth this; and if so be it shall be driven intensely or remissly, it will work after the same manner in the matter. The Information of the whole Work dependeth of the measure of External Fire.

101. He that is ignorant of the degrees and points of external Fire, let him not start upon the Philosophical Work; for he will never obtain light out of darkness, unless the heats pass through their middle stages, like the Elements, whose Extremes are not converted, but only their Means.

102. Because the whole work consisteth in Separation and perfect Preparation of the Four Elements, therefore so many

grades of Fire are necessary thereunto; for every Element is extracted by the degree of Fire proper to it.

103. The four grades of Heat are called the heat of the Water Bath, the heat of Ashes, of Coals, and of Flame, which is also called "Optetic:" every grade hath its degrees, two at least, sometimes three; for heat is to be moved slowly and by degrees, whether it be increased or decreased; so that Matter, after Nature's example, may go on by degrees and willingly unto formation and completion; for nothing is so strange to Nature as that which is violent. Let the Philosopher propound for his consideration the gentle access and recess of the Sun, whose Light and Lamp bestoweth its heat to the things of the world, according to the times and Laws of the Universe, and so bestoweth a certain temperament upon them.

104. The first degree of the Bath of Heat is called the heat of a Fever; the second, of Dung. The first degree of the second grade is the simple heat of Ashes, the second is the heat of Sand. Now the degrees of Fire, Coals and Flame want a proper Name, but they are distinguished by the operation of the intellect, according to their intensity [and remission].

105. Three grades only of Fire are sometimes found amongst Philosophers, *viz.*, the Water Bath, of Ashes and of Flame: which latter comprehendeth the Fire of Coals and of Flame: the Heat of Dung is sometimes distinguished from the Heat of the Bath in degree. Thus for the most part Authors do involve the light in darkness, by the various expressions of the Philosophers' Fire; for the knowledge thereof is accounted amongst their chief secrets.

106. In the White Work, because three Elements only are extracted, Three degrees of Fire do suffice; the last, to wit the "Optetic," is reserved for the Fourth Element, which finisheth the Red Work. By the first degree the eclipse of Sol and Luna is made; by the second the light of Luna begins to be restored; by the third Luna attaineth unto the fullness of

her splendour; and by the fourth Sol is exalted into the highest apex of his glory. Now in every part the Fire is administered according to the rules of Geometry; so that the Agent may answer to the disposition of the Patient, and their strength be equally poised betwixt themselves.

107. Philosophers have very much insisted upon secrecy in regard to their Fire, they scarce have been bold to describe it, but shew it rather by a description of its qualities and properties, than by its name: as that it is called Airy Fire, Vaporous, Humid and Dry, Clear or Star-like; because it may easily by degrees be increased or remitted as the Artificer pleaseth. He that desireth more of the knowledge of Fire may be satisfied by the Works of Lullius,[51] who hath opened the Secrets of Practice to worthy minds candidly.

108. Of the conflict of the Eagle and the Lion also they write diversely, because the Lion is the strongest animal, and therefore it is necessary that more Eagles act together (three at least, or more, even to ten) to conquer him: the fewer they are, the greater the contention, and the slower the Victory; but the more Eagles, the shorter the Battle, and the plundering of the Lion will more readily follow. The happier number of seven Eagles may be taken out of Lullius, or of nine out of Senior.[52]

109. The Vessel wherein Philosophers decoct their work is twofold; the one of Nature, the other of Art; the Vessel of Nature which is also called the Vessel of Philosophy is the Earth of the Stone, or the Female or Matrix, whereinto the sperm of the Male is received, putrefies, and is prepared for generation; the Vessel of Nature is of three sorts, for the secret is decocted in a threefold Vessel.

110. The First Vessel is made of a transparent Stone, or of a stony Glass, the form thereof some Philosophers have hid by a certain Enigmatic description; sometimes affirming that it is compounded of two pieces, to wit, an Alembic and

a Bolt-head; sometimes of three, at other times of the two former with the addition of a Cover.

111. Many have feigned the multiplying of such like Vessels to be necessary to the Philosophical Work, calling them by divers names with a desire of hiding the secret by a diversity of operations; for they called it Dissolvent of solutions; Putrefactory for putrefaction; Distillatory for distillation; Sublimatory for sublimetion; Calcinatory for calcination, *etc.*

112. But all deceit being removed we may speak sincerely, one only Vessel of Art sufficeth to terminate the Work of either Sulphur; and another for the Work of the Elixir; for the diversity of digestions requireth not the change of Vessels; yea we must have a care lest the Vessel be changed or opened before the First work be ended.

113. You shall choose a form of glass Vessel round in the bottom (or cucurbit), or at least oval, the neck a hand's breadth long or more, large enough, with a straight mouth made like a Pitcher or Jug, continuous and unbroken and equally thick in every part, that it may resist a long, and sometimes an acute Fire: The cucurbit is called a Blind-head because its eye is blinded with the Hermetic seal, lest anything from without should enter in, or the Spirit steal out.

114. The second Vessel of Art may be of Wood, of the trunk of an Oak, cut into two hollow Hemispheres, wherein the Philosophers' Egg may be cherished till it be hatched; of which see the Fountain of Trevisan.[53]

115. The third Vessel Practitioners have called their Furnace, which keeps the other Vessels with the matter and the whole work: this also Philosophers have endeavoured to hide amongst their secrets.

116. The Furnace which is the Keeper of Secrets, is called Athanor, from the immortal Fire, which it always preserveth; for although it afford unto the Work continual

Fire, yet sometimes unequally, which reason requireth to be administered more or less according to the quantity of matter, and the capacity of the Furnace.

117. The matter of the Furnace is made of Brick, or of daubed Earth, or of Potter's clay well beaten and prepared with horse dung, mixed with hair, so that it may cohere the firmer, and may not be cracked by long heating; let the walls be three or four fingers thick, to the end that the furnace may be the better able to keep in the heat and withstand it.

118. Let the form of the Furnace be round, the inward altitude of two feet or thereabouts, in the midst whereof an Iron or Brazen plate must be set, of a round Figure, about the thickness of a Penknife's back, in a manner possessing the interior latitude of the Furnace, but a little narrower than it, lest it touch the walls; it must lean upon three or four props of Iron fixed to the walls, and let it be full of holes, that the heat may be the more easily carried upwards by them, and between the sides of the Furnace and the Plate. Below the Plate let there be a little door left, and another above in the walls of the Furnace, that by the Lower the Fire may be put in, and by the higher the temperament of the heat may be sensibly perceived; at the opposite part whereof let there be a little window of the Figure of a Rhomboid fortified with glass, that the light over against it may shew the colours to the eye. Upon the middle of the aforesaid plate, let the Tripod of secrets be placed with a double Vessel. Lastly, let the Furnace be very well covered with a shell or covering agreeable unto it, and take care that the little doors be always closely shut, lest the heat escape.

119. Thus thou hast all things necessary to the First Work, the end whereof is the generation of two sorts of Sulphur; the composition and perfection of both may be thus finished.

[The Practice of the Sulphur:] ℞. [Praxis:] Take a Red Dragon, courageous, warlike, to whom no natural strength is wanting; and afterwards seven or nine noble Eagles (Virgins), whose eyes will not wax dull by the rays of the Sun: cast the Birds with the Beast into a clear Prison and strongly shut them up; under this let a Bath be placed, that they may be incensed to fight by the warmth; in a short time they will enter into a long and harsh contention, until at length about the 45th day or the 50th the Eagles begin to prey upon and tear the beast to pieces, which dying will infect the whole Prison with its black and direful poison, whereby the Eagles being wounded, they will also be constrained to give up the ghost. From the putrefaction of the dead Carcasses a Crow will be generated, which by little and little will put forth its head, and the Heat being somewhat increased it will forthwith stretch forth its wings and begin to fly; but seeking chinks from the Winds and Clouds, it will long hover about; take heed that it find not any chinks. At length being made white by a gentle and long Rain, and with the dew of Heaven it will be changed into a White Swan, but the new born Crow is a sign of the departed Dragon. In making the Crow White, extract the Elements, and distil them according to the order prescribed, until they be fixed in their Earth, and end in Snow-like and most subtle dust, which being finished thou shalt enjoy thy first desire, the White Work.

120. If thou intendest to proceed further to the Red, add the Element of Fire, which is not needed for the White Work: the Vessel therefore being fixed, and the Fire strengthened by little and little through its grades, force the matter until the occult begin to be made manifest, the sign whereof will be the Orange colour arising: raise the Fire to the Fourth degree by its degrees, until by the help of Vulcan, purple Roses be generated from the Lily, and lastly the Amaranth dyed with the dark Redness of blood: but thou mayest not cease to

bring out Fire by Fire, until thou shalt behold the matter terminated in most Red ashes, imperceptible to the touch. This Red Stone may rear up thy mind to greater things, by the blessing and assistance of the holy Trinity.

121. They that think they have brought their work to an end by perfect Sulphur, not knowing Nature or Art, and to have fulfilled the Precepts of the secret, are much deceived, and will try Projection in vain; for the Praxis of the Stone is perfected by a double Work; the First is the creation of the Sulphur; the Second is the making of the Elixir.

122. The aforesaid Philosophers' Sulphur is most subtle Earth, most hot and dry, in the belly whereof the Fire of Nature abundantly multiplied is hidden. Therefore it deserveth the name of the Fire of the Stone, for it hath in itself the virtue of opening and penetrating the bodies of Metals, and of turning them into its own temperament and producing its like, wherefore it is called a Father and Masculine seed.

123. That we may leave nothing untouched, let the Students in Philosophy know that from that first Sulphur, a second is generated which may be multiplied *ad infinitum:* let the wise man, after he hath got the everlasting mineral of that Heavenly Fire, keep it diligently. Now of what matter Sulphur is generated, of the same it is multiplied, a small portion of the first being added, yet as in the Balance. The rest, a tyro may see in Lullius,[54] it may suffice only to point to this.

124. The Elixir is compounded of a threefold matter, namely, of Metallic Water or Mercury sublimated as before; of Leaven White or Red, according to the intention of the Operator; and of the Second Sulphur, all by Weight.

125. There are Five proper and necessary qualities in the perfect Elixir, that it be fusible, permanent, penetrating, tincturing, and multiplying; it borroweth its tincture and fixation from the Leaven; its penetration from the

Sulphur; its fusion from Argent vive, which is the medium of conjoining Tinctures; to wit of the Ferment and Sulphur; and its multiplicative virtue from the Spirit infused into the Quintessence.

126. Two perfect Metals give a perfect Tincture, because they are dyed with the pure Sulphur of Nature, and therefore no Ferment of Metals may be sought except these two bodies; therefore dye thy Elixir White and Red with Luna and Sol; Mercury first of all receives their Tincture, and having received it, doth communicate it to others.

127. In compounding the Elixir take heed you change not or mix anything with the Ferments, for either Elixir must have its proper Ferment, and desireth its proper Elements; for it is provided by Nature that the two Luminaries have their different Sulphurs and distinct tinctures.

128. The Second work is concocted as the First, in the same or a like Vessel, the same Furnace, and by the same degrees of fire, but is perfected in a shorter time.

129. There are three humours in the Stone, which are to be extracted successively; namely, Watery, Airy, and Radical; and therefore all the labour and care of the Workman is employed about the humour, neither is any other Element in the Work of the Stone, circulated, besides the humid one. For it is necessary, in the first place, that the Earth be resolved and melted into humour. Now the Radical humour of all things, accounted Fire, is most tenacious, because it is tied to the Centre of Nature, from which it is not easily separated; extract, therefore, these three humours slowly and successively; dissolving and congealing them by their Wheels, for by the multiplied alternative reiteration of Solution and Congelation the Wheel is extended and the whole work finished.

130. The Elixir's perfection consisteth in the strict Union and indissoluble Matrimony of *Siccum* and *Humidum*, so that

they may not be separated, but the *Siccum* may flow with moderate heat into the *Humidum*, abiding every pressure of Fire. The sign of perfection is that if a very little of it be cast in above the Iron or Brazen Plate while very hot, it flow forthwith without smoke.

131. ℞. [Praxis:] Let three weights of Red Earth or of Red Ferment, and a double weight of Water and Air, well ground up, be mixed together. Let an Amalgama be made like Butter, or Metalline Paste, so that the Earth being mollified may be insensible to the touch. Add one weight and a half of Fire; let these be transferred to the Vessel and exposed to a Fire of the first degree; most closely sealed; afterwards let the Elements be extracted out of their degrees of Fire in their order, which being turned downwards with a gentle motion they may be fixed in their Earth, so as nothing Volatile may be raised up from thence; the matter at length shall be terminated in a Stone, Illuminated, Red and Diaphanous; a part whereof take at pleasure, and having cast it into a Crucible with a little Fire by drops give it to drink its Red Oil and incerate it,[55] until it be quite melted, and do flow without smoke. Nor mayest thou fear its flight, for the Earth being mollified with the sweetness of the Potion will retain it, having received it, within its bowels: then take the Elixir thus perfected into thine own power and keep it carefully. In God rejoice, and be silent.

132. The order and method of composing and perfecting the white Elixir is the same, so that thou usest the white Elements only in the composition thereof; but the body of it brought to the term of decoction will end in the plate; white, splendid, and crystal-like, which incerated with its White Oil will be fused. Cast one weight of either Elixir, upon ten times its weight of Argent vive well washed and thou wilt admire its effect with astonishment.

133. Because in the Elixir the strength of Natural Fire is most abundantly multiplied by the Spirit infused into the Quintessence, and the depraved accidents of bodies, which beset their purity and the true light of Nature with darkness, are taken away by long and manifold sublimations and digestions; therefore Fiery Nature freed from its Fetters and fortified with the aid of Heavenly strength, works most powerfully, being included in this our Fifth Element: let it not therefore be a wonder, if it obtain strength not only to perfect imperfect things, but also to multiply its force and power. Now the Fountain of Multiplication is in the Prince of the Luminaries, who by the infinite multiplication of his beams, begetteth all things in this our Orb, and multiplieth things generated, by infusing a multiplicative virtue into the seeds of things.

134. The way of multiplying the Elixir is threefold: By the first; ℞. [Praxis:] Mingle one weight of Red Elixir, with nine times its weight of Red Water, and dissolve it into Water in a Vessel suitable for Solution; the matter being well dissolved and united coagulate it by decoction with a gentle Fire, until it be made strong into a Ruby or Red Lamel, which afterwards incerate with its Red Oil, after the manner prescribed until it melt and flow; so shalt thou have a medicine ten times more powerful than the first. The business is easily finished in a short time.

135. By the Second manner. ℞. [Praxis:] What Portion thou pleasest of thy Elixir mixed with its Water, the weights being observed; seal it very well in the Vessel of Reduction, dissolve it in a Bath, by inhumation; being dissolved, distil it, separating the Elements by their proper degrees of fire, and fixing them downwards, as was done in the first and second work, until it become a Stone; lastly, incerate it and Project it. This is the longer, but yet the richer way, for the virtue of the Elixir is increased even an hundred fold; for by how much the

more subtle it is made by reiterated operations, so much more both of superior and inferior strength it retaineth, and more powerfully operateth.

136. Lastly, take one Ounce of the said Elixir multiplied in virtue, and project it upon an hundred of purified Mercury, and in a little time the Mercury made hot amongst burning Coals, will be converted into pure Elixir; whereof if thou castest every ounce upon another hundred of the like Mercury, Sol will shine most purely to thine eyes. The multiplication of White Elixir may be made in the same way. Study the virtues of this Medicine to cure all kinds of diseases, and to preserve good health, as also other uses thereof, out of the Writings of Arnold of Villa Nova,[56] Lullius and of other Philosophers.

137. The Significator of the Philosopher will instruct him concerning the Times of the Stone, for the first Work "ad Album" [to white] must be terminated in the House of Luna; the Second, in the second House of Mercury. The first Work "ad Rubeum" [to red], will end in the Second House of Venus, and the last in the other Regal Throne of Jupiter, from whence our most Potent King shall receive a Crown decked with most precious Rubies:

> Sic in se sua vestigia volvitur Annus.
>
> Thus doth the winding of the circling Year
> Trace its own Foot-steps, and the same appear.

138. A Three-Headed Dragon keepeth this Golden Fleece; the first Head proceedeth from the Waters, the second from the Earth, the third from the Air; it is necessary that these three heads do end in One most Potent, which will devour all the other Dragons; then a way is laid open for thee to the Golden Fleece. Farewell! diligent Reader; in Reading these things invocate the Spirit of Eternal Light; Speak little, Meditate much, and Judge aright.[57]

## The Times of the Stone.[†]

The interpretation of The Philosophers' Signifïcator. To every Planet two Houses were assigned by the Ancients, Sol and Luna excepted; whereof the planet Saturn hath his two houses adjoining. Philosophers in handling their Philosophical work, begin their years in Winter, to wit; the Sun being in Capricorn, which is the former House of Saturn; and so come towards the right hand. In the Second place the other House of Saturn is found in Aquarius, at which time Saturn, *i.e.*, the Blackness of the work of the Magistery begins after the forty-fifth or fiftieth day. Sol coming into Pisces the work is black, blacker than black, and the head of the Crow begins to appear. The third month being ended, and Sol entering into Aries, the sublimation or separation of the Elements begin. Those which follow unto Cancer make the Work White. Cancer addeth the greatest whiteness and splendour, and doth perfectly fill up all the days of the Stone, or white Sulphur, or the Lunar work of Sulphur; Luna sitting and reigning gloriously in her House. In Leo, the Regal Mansion of the Sun, the Solar work begins, which in Libra is terminated into a Ruby Stone or perfect Sulphur. The two signs Scorpio and Sagittarius which remain are required for the completing of the Elixir. And thus the Philosophers' admirable offspring taketh its beginning in the Reign of Saturn, and its end and perfection in the Dominion of Jupiter.

---

Note:

†. Westcott reprinted this from the *Arcanum, or Great Secret of Hermetic Philosophy*, and published in *Fasciculus Chemicus, or Chymical Collections*. Translated by James Hasolle [Elias Ashmole], 1650. "The Times of the Stone" was not in the original 1623 edition.—D.K.

# NOTES

TO THE

# "HERMETIC ARCANUM."

---

1. Due reverence for Divine powers is an absolute necessity in the search for occult wisdom, and can alone lead any student in safety to success in the arts of High Magic.

2. Theosophic Eastern teaching (as well as Western Hermetic ritual) insists upon mental and moral as well as bodily purity in every candidate for esoteric instruction.

3. A warning that complete success can hardly be achieved, unless the student is able to devote himself entirely to the pursuit of the occult sciences. *Non omnia possumus omnes* [We can't all do everything].

4. A warning against spiritual pride; the besetting sin of one who has gone up some steps of the mystic ladder, and who realizes for the first time that there is something he can teach, as well as so much that he has to learn.

5. "Orare est laborare" [To pray is to work] is the true motto of the Hermetist. Work inspired by enthusiasm and the will to progress, so as to fit oneself to raise others, is ideal prayer in action.

6. If you freely receive knowledge and power you must freely give: the epigram attributed to a fellow student was, "I give, I give; but the more I give, the more do I receive."

7. James i. 27, "Keep himself unspotted from the world," it is more easy to remain clean away from a dirty world; yet if one can keep clean amid the turmoil of a city,

such conduct is deserving of a higher reward than is due to a clean but ascetic life.

8. In tranquillity alone can meditation be fertile the flower can only bloom in the calm after the violence of the storm of contest with the passions.

9. In peaceful meditation is the opportunity of that aspiration to the Divine which *may* lead to union (even if momentary) with the Higher and Divine Genius—the Light that *may* light every man that cometh into the world.

10. A teacher and guide is almost an absolute necessity in the Higher Magic; not to drag on the pupil, but to point out the path that has been trodden with success, and to warn against tempting bye-paths with meretricious attractions, but "whose splendour is but seeming." Among the Rosicrucians each Adept was authorized and encouraged to choose one or more pupils to follow in his steps and to take up the mantle and wand when his time came to lay them down.

11. Apart from the help of a Master, it is nearly always found that a fellow student is a great help to progress. A few there are who succeed most in solitary study; others are much helped by the presence of a responsive zeal and reflected desire. A trio of students has also a certain advantage. History has but few examples of two fellow students of the same sex achieving great results: but there are many instances of great progress and high results from the combined work of a truly high minded woman and man developing by mutual and reciprocal interaction; the female providing knowledge by intuition, and the male formulating and developing the practical aspect of the matter. Even in the preliminary grades of mystic study the same result is obtained: unrestrained and unconventional social and intellectual communion may (in the absolute absence of passion) lead to rapid mental and spiritual progress. Compare the narratives of Moses and Miriam, Paul and Thecla, Theon and Hypatia, Flamel and Pernelle, Gichtel and Sophia, Anna Kingsford and her still

living *collaborateur* [*i.e.*, Edward Maitland]. Analogy supports the proposition, through all the forms of the manifested universe; wherever the Dyad is developed, the presence of the contrasted forces alone leads to a due result.

12. Beware of false guides: perhaps it is wisest to add, follow only one path at once; even if it be granted that two parallel paths exist, and that they meet farther on—yet it is most easy to attempt one only; still the attempt to traverse both at once is not absolutely forbidden, either by the chiefs of the Western or Eastern Schools.

13. Whenever a student happens upon a very definite assertion in a book certainly the work of a high adept, it is generally safe to seek further; for the ancient writers, when they did publish, never threw pearls of learning away, although willing to tender them to earnest students.

14. Michael Sendivogius; the anonymous inscription on his books was "Author sum qui *Divi Leschi Genus Amo.*" The last four words form an anagram of his name; he flourished 1604-46; his chief works are *Novum Lumen Chymicum, De Sulphure, Lucerna Salis, de Lapide, Dialogus Mercurii* and *Epistolæ.*

15. Flamel's work, *The Hieroglyphical Figures, which he caused to be Painted upon an Arch in St. Innocents Church Yard in Paris*, has been reprinted with a preface by W. Wynn Westcott. Nicolas Flamel flourished 1357-1413.

16. See Virgil. *Æneid* vi. 138. The original has "*hunc*" not "*quem.*"

17. Virgil. *Æneid* vi. 190-193.

18. See the *Chrysopœia* of Aurelius Augurellus, liber x.; this author died 1514.

19. By these words is meant that the chemical substances used should be quite pure, otherwise the adulterations will hinder the desired result.

20. Probably meaning freshly prepared; perhaps what the modern chemist calls "in a nascent state."

21. Death, the inevitable changer, Siva.

22. In almost all cases where sexual symbolism is used, any principle which is positive to that which is inferior, is also negative or female to that which is superior.

23. These names vary with different authors:—
Gabritius is also called Gabertius and Gabricus. Beia also is Beya. As brother and sister they mean positive and negative. See David Laqueus. *Harmonia Chemica*; and the dicta of Arislæus in the *Turba Philosophorum*. Gabritius is the fixed and Beia the volatile.

24. Raymond Lully. *Prior Testamentum*, cap. 62.

25. See Note 19.

26. Hosea vii. 9.

27. The rocks of Scylla and the whirlpool of Charybdis lie on either side of the strait between Sicily and Italy.

28. Query, dissolved.

29. *Rebis* is generally explained as that which is "double," or is hermaphrodite, or is the result of the union of two substances.

30. Virgil. *Æneid* vi. 129, 130.

31. The planet Mercury is said in Astrology to act by influence upon other planets in aspect with it, rather than with independent force.

32. See the *Chrysopœia* of Augurellus, 2.

33. Ensigns of Diana and the Doves of Venus: query purity and love on the spiritual plane; or is the reference to Silver on the material plane. For some notes on Alchymy on the spiritual plane, see *Alchymy*, by Sapere Aude.

34. Virgil. *Georgics*, Book I., lines 64, 65, 44.

35. See Cap. 4, libr. I., of the *Perfect Magistery* of Geber; he lived about a.d. 830.

36. See Genesis i. verses 1 to 4.

37. See Deut. xxxiii. v. 13 to 16. These words differ from the version of the English Bible. For "apples of Heaven," read "precious things." For "the apple of fruit both of the sun and moon," read "the precious fruits brought forth by the sun, and the precious things put forth by the moon." For "the top," read "the chief things." The Hebrew word translated "apple" is MGD. Parkhurst gives "precious fruits." The Hebrew word for "top" or "chief things" is RASh, meaning head, chief or beginning. Godfrey Higgins laboured to teach that it also meant "wisdom:" it is the first word of Genesis, preceded by a Beth – B-RAShITh.

38. This means adulteration, impurity from its mineral origin.

39. Or interstitial, intimately combined with it; yet such as can be easily driven off by a suitable heat.

40. Compare this purple Jovian star with the purple flower of love, the Amaranth in paragraph 53. There is a scale of colours in which Jupiter is Violet.

41. A versification of this beautiful passage may be found in Ainsworth, as spoken by the Sylph appearing to Ruggieri.

42. Note the change from she to he, negative to positive in this paragragh. Nothing is more realistic than sexual symbolism, but one has to exclude it as far as possible for the sake of the Pharisee reader.

43. Let the practical Alchymist note this word, and indeed the whole paragraph, and remember that there is *a* butter besides butter.

44. That is twilight, gloom of evening, the first darkening.

45. Virgil. *Georgics*. I., 70.

46. Virgil. *Georgics*. I., 47.

47. That is "moist" and "dry."

48. Note this order–earth, water, air, fire; and back to earth. See end of paragraph 79.

49. See the *Enchiridion* in Manget's *Bibliotheca*, liber. III., section 3.

50. From *humus* the ground, earth or soil.

51. Raymond Lully was martyred in Africa, 1315.

52. Senior: very little is known of this author; his name is not in the list of Lenglet de Fresnoy.

53. Bernard, Count of Treves; died about 1490. His chief works are, *Natural Philosophy of Metals*, *The Secret Work of Chymia*, and *La Parole délaissée*.

54. His most valued works are *Lullii Testamentum, Codicillus seu Vade Mecum aut Cantilena* and *Practica*.

55. Definition of some terms. Inceration must not be confused with incineration, which means reducing to ashes by means of heat. Inceration implies the gradual addition of a liquid (as our mercury) to a solid powder (as our sulphur), until the mixture is of the consistence of *wax*, of which the Latin word is *cera*. See Martin Rulandus *A Lexicon of Alchemy*, (1893).

Cohobation is a process of continuous volatilization and condensation of a volatile liquid in a closed vessel subjected to heat.

Anger: when it is written that you are not to provoke anger, it is meant, do not overheat the matter.

The Goose of Hermogenes is the solvent of the Philosophers, which Bernard of Treves calls the Gate of the Palace of the King.

56. Arnold of Villanova, died 1310; his chief works are *Novum Lumen, Flos Florum, Rosarium, Liber Perfectionis, Speculum Alchymiæ*, and *Arcanum Philosophicum*.

57. The original Latin work ends with paragraph 138; the English edition of Elias Ashmole has an additional chapter by I.C. Chymierastes: this has no Alchymic value and is but an apology for Hermes, that he was not a Christian.

# APPENDIX I:

## TO THE LOVERS OF

## "HERMETIC PHILOSOPHY,"

by I.C. Chymierastes

*wisheth prosperity.*†

---

SUCH is the difference between the Hermetics' living Philosophy, and, the dead Philosophy of the Ethnics; that the former hath been Divinely inspired into the first Masters of Chymistry (the Queen of all Sciences,) and therefore may challenge the Holy Spirit of Truth for its only Author; who by breathing where he listeth, doth infuse the true Light of Nature into their minds; by virtue whereof, all the darkness of errors is straight-ways chased away from thence and utterly expelled: but the latter may ascribe its Invention unto Pagans, who having left, or rather neglected the pure Fountains of Learning, have introduced false Principles and causes, (proceeding from their own brain) for true ones, to the great damage of the Republic of Learning. And indeed what good were they able to do, upon whom the Day-Star of Truth, the Eternal Wisdom of God, the Fountain of all Knowledge and Understanding *Christ Jesus* hath never risen? We cannot wonder therefore, that they have only proposed old wives Fables, and foolish toys, that they have introduced pure dotages, and innumerable inventions of lies, whereby they have so bedaubed holy Philosophy, that we can find nothing of Native-beauty in it.

But you will object that *Hermes* himself the Prince of Vital Philosophy was an Heathen also, yea and lived before other Authors many ages, by whose decrees Philosophy in every place entertained, with greatest applause of almost all men, now flourisheth. But granting that, what followeth? This *Hermes Trismegistus* indeed was born in an Heathen Country, yet by a peculiar privilege is from God he was one, who worshipped the true God in his life, manners and Religion especially; who freely confessed God the Father, and that he was the Creator of Man, and made no other partaker of Divinity with him: He acknowledged the Son of God the Father, by whom all things which are existent, were made; whose name because it was wonderful and ineffable, was unknown to Men, and even to Angels themselves, who admire with astonishment his generation. What more? He was our *Hermes* who by the singular indulgence and revelation at the most great and gracious God, foreknew that the same Son should come in the Flesh, and that in the last ages, to the end he might bless the Godly forever. He it was who so clearly taught, that the mystery of the most Holy Trinity ought to be adored, as well in the Plurality of Persons, as in the unity of Divine Essence, in three Hypostasis, (as any quick-sighted and intelligent man may gather from that which follows;) as that it can scarcely be found anywhere more clearly and plainly: for thus he: *There was an Intelligent Light before the Intelligent Light, and there was always a clear Mind of the Mind: and the Truth hereof, and the Spirit containing all things, was no other thing: Besides this God is not, nor Angel, nor any other Essence; for he is Lord of all, both Father, and God, all things are under him, and in him, I beseech thee O Heaven, and the wise work of the great God; I beseech thee thou voice of the Father, which he first spake, when he formed the whole world: I beseech thee by the only begotten Word, and Father containing all things, be propitious unto me.*

Now ye Sons of *Hermes,* turnover and over again, both night and day the Volumes of Heathen Philosophers, and inquire with what diligence you possibly can, whether you are able to find such Holy, such Godly and Catholic things in them.

Our *Hermes* was an Heathen, I confess, yet such an Heathen as knew the power and greatness of God, by other creatures and also by himself, and glorified God, as God: I shall not spare to add, that he far excelled in godliness most Christians now a days in name only; and gave immortal thanks unto him as the Fountain of all good things, with a deep submission of mind for his benefits received. Hear I pray, ye sons of Learning, whether God was as much conversant, and wrought as equally in the Heathen Nation, as amongst his own people, when he saith: *From the rising of the Sun unto the going down thereof his name is great amongst the Gentiles; and in every place a pure oblation is sacrificed and offered unto my name, because my name is great amongst the Nations, saith the Lord of Hosts by his Prophet.*

Rub up your memory, I entreat you, and speak plainly; were not the *Magi* Heathens, which came from the East by the guidance of a Star, that they might worship Christ, whom nevertheless the unbelieving people hanged upon a Tree. Lastly consider well I beseech you, ye faithful favourers of true Wisdom only; from what Fountain other Heathens besides *Hermes* have taken the Principles of their Learning. Wear and better wear out their Volumes with diligence, that ye may discern them to refer their wisdom not unto God, but to attribute it, as gotten by their own Industry. On the contrary cast your eyes upon the beginning of the admirable Tractate having seven Chapters of your Father *Hermes* concerning the Secret of the *Physical Stone,* and observe how holily he thinketh of God the bestower of this Secret Science: for *Hermes* saith: *In so great an Age I have not ceased to try experiments, nor have I spared my Soul from labour: I had this Art and Science by the Inspiration of the Living God only, who hath vouchsafed to open it to me his servant. 'Tis true, he hath given power of judging to rational creatures, but hath not left unto any an occasion of sinning. But I, unless I feared the day of*

*Doom, or the souls damnation for the concealing of this Science; I would make known nothing of this Science, nor* prophetize *to any. But I have been willing to render to the Faithful their due, as the Author of Faith hath been pleased to bestow upon me.*

Thus *Hermes:* then which nothing could have ever been said more wise, or more agreeable to Christian Religion. And hence it is, that so many as are or have been of a more sublime wit and manly judgment, have embraced the Living, Holy, and Divine Philosophy of *Hermes,* with all their Soul and Strength (rejecting that dead, profane, and humane Philosophy of the *Ethnics)* and have commended and illustrated it in divers of their Writings and Watchings. Of all which, that I may confess ingenuously, seeing that I could never read unto this day any Writer more true, neat, and clear, than the Author of this Tractate, *Anonymous* indeed, yet one that truly deserves the name of an Adepted Philosopher; I have thought it worth my pains, and have deemed hereby to confer not the least favour upon the sons of *Hermes,* if I shall again publish the hidden Work of *Hermetic Philosophy,* with the *Philosophers Signifer,* according to the intention of this most wise Author.

*FAREWELL.*

Note:

†. Reprinted from the *Arcanum, or Great Secret of Hermetic Philosophy,* and published in *Fasciculus Chemicus, or Chymical Collections.* Translated by James Hasolle [Elias Ashmole], 1650. The Text has been modernized to match Westcott's translation.–D.K.

# APPENDIX II:

## THE TIMES OF THE *STONE*.[†]

The Figure described is the Philosophers *Signifer*.[‡] To every Planet a double House is assigned by the Ancients, *Sol* and *Luna* excepted; whereof everyone borroweth one House only, both of them adjoining. In the said Figure every Planet possesseth its proper Houses. Philosophers in handling their Philosophical work, begin their year in Winter, to wit, the Sun being in *Capricorn*, which is the former House of *Saturn*; and so come towards the right hand. In the Second place the other House of *Saturn* is found in *Aquarius*, at which time *Saturn*, *i.e.*, the Blackness of the Dominary work begins after the forty-fifth or fiftieth day. *Sol* coming into *Pisces* the work is black, blacker than black, and the head of the Crow begins to appear.[2] The third month being ended, and *Sol* entering into *Aries*, the sublimation or separation of the Elements begins. Those which follow unto *Cancer* make the Work White. *Cancer* addeth the greatest whiteness and splendour, and doth perfectly fill up all the days of the Stone, or white Sulphur, or the Lunar work of Sulphur, *Luna* sitting and reigning gloriously in her House. In *Leo*, the Regal Mansion of the Sun, the Solar work begins, which in *Libra* is terminated into a Ruby Stone, or perfect Sulphur. The two signs *Scorpio* and *Sagittarius* which remain, are indebted to the completing of the Elixir. And thus the Philosophers' admirable young taketh its beginning in the Reign of *Saturn*, and its end and perfection in the Dominion of *Jupiter*.

## *The Signifer of Philosophers with the Houses of the Planets.*

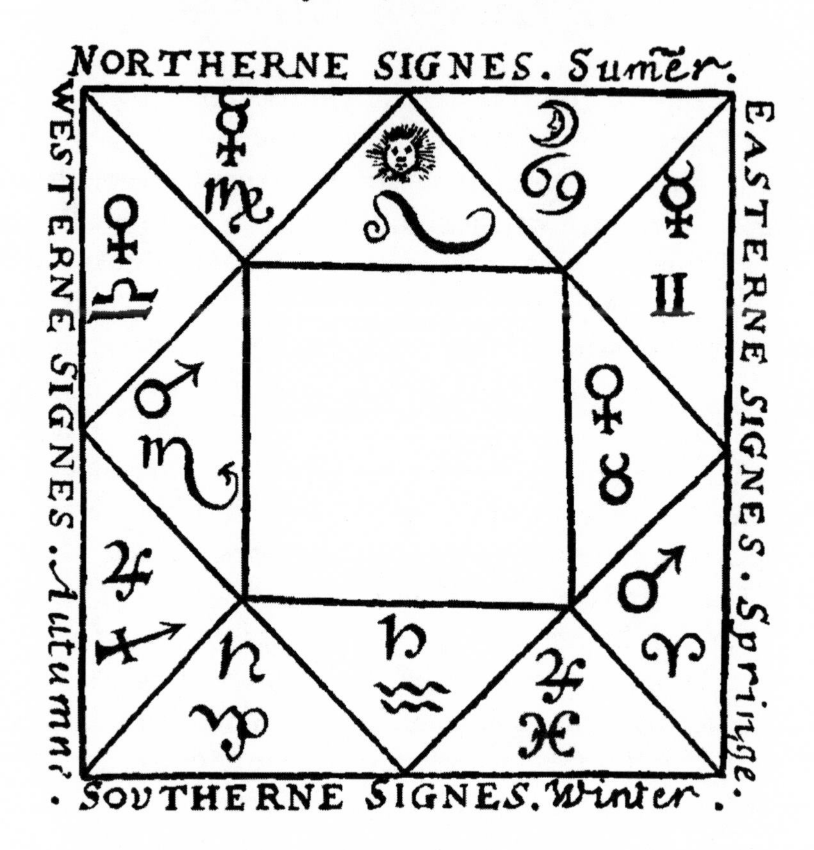


*FINIS.*

Notes:

†. Reprinted from the *Arcanum, or Great Secret of Hermetic Philosophy*, and published in *Fasciculus Chemicus, or Chymical Collections*. Translated by James Hasolle [Elias Ashmole], 1650. The Text has been modernized to match Westcott's translation.—D.K.

‡. The Interpretation of the Philosophers' Scheme.—J.H.

# APPENDIX III:

## POSTSCRIPT.[†]

*AFTER I had written this Preface, and committed it to the Press, I happily met with the following* Arcanum, *and perceiving it to suit so punctually with these* Chymical Collections, *for the solidity, likeness, and bravery of the* Matter *and* Form, *and to confirm some of those Directions, Cautions, and Admonitions I had laid down in the* Prolegomena; *and withal, finding it a piece of very* Eminent Learning *and* Regard, *I adventured to translate it likewise, and persuaded the Printer to join them into one* Book *which I hope will not dislike the* Reader *nor overcharge the* Buyer: *And though in the* Translation *thereof, I have used the same solemnity and reservation, as in the former, and such as befits so venerable and transcendent a* Secret: *Yet I hope, that those who (favored with a propitious* Birth) *search into the Sacred Remains of* Ancient Learning, *admire the rare and disguised effects of* Nature, *and through their* Piety *and* Honesty, *become worthy of it, may find* Ariadnes *thread to conduct them through the delusive windings of this intricate* Labyrinth.

1. April, 1650.

James Hasolle.

Notes:

†. This is Elias Ashmole's explanation of why he added a translation of the *Arcanum* to his translation of Arthur Dee's *Fasciculus Chemicus, or Chymical Collections.* The Postscript follows his Preface or "Prolegomena," and is dated 1 March 1650. The Text has been modernized to match Westcott's translation.—D.K.

# APPENDIX IV:

## THE RESTORED LUNAR WORK.†

19. Most Philosophers have affirmed that their Kingly Work is wholly composed of the Sun and Moon; others have thought good to add Mercury to the Sun: some have chosen Sulphur and Mercury; others have attributed no small part in so great a Work to Salt mingled with the other two. The very same men have professed that this clear Stone is made of one thing only, sometimes of two, other times of three, at other times of four, and of five; and thus though writing so variously upon the same subject, do nevertheless agree in sense and meaning.

20. Now that (abandoning all Cheats) we may deal candidly and truly, we hold that this entire Work is perfected by two Bodies only; to wit, by Sun and Moon rightly prepared, for this is the mere generation which is by nature, with the help of Art, wherein the population of male and female doth intercede, and from whence an offspring far more noble than the Parents is brought forth.

21. Now those Bodies must be taken, which are of an unspotted and incorrupt virginity; such as have life and spirit in them; not extinct as those that are handled by the vulgar; for who can expect life from dead things; and those are called corrupt which have suffered combination; those dead and extinct which (by the enforcement of the chief Tyrant of the world) have poured out their soul with their blood by Martyrdom; fly a fratricide from whom the greatest imminent danger in the whole Work is threatened.

22. The Sun is Masculine, forasmuch as it sendeth forth active and enforcing seed; the Moon is Feminine, called the matrix and vessel of Nature, because she receiveth the seed of the male in her womb, and fostereth it by her monthly provision yet doth it not altogether want its active virtue; for, first of all (being ravished with love) she climbs up unto the male, until she hath wrested from him the utmost delights of *Venus*, and fruitful seed: nor doth she desist from her embraces, till that being great with child, she slip gently away.

23. By the name of Moon Philosophers understand not the vulgar Moon, which is also masculine in its operation, and in copulation acts the part of a male. Let none therefore presume to try the wicked and unnatural conjunction of two males, neither let him conceive any hope of issue from such copulation, but he shall join *Gabritius* to *Beia*, and offer the sister to her won brother in firm Matrimony, that from thence he may receive Sol's noble Son.

24. They that hold Sulphur and Mercury to be the Matter of the Stone, by the name of Sulphur, they understand Sun and common Moon; by Mercury the Philosophic Moon; so (without dissimulation) holy Lullius adviseth his friend, that he attempt not to work without Mercury and Luna for Silver; and Mercury and Sol for Gold.

25. Let none therefore be deceived by adding a third to two: for Love admitteth not a third; and wedlock is terminated in the number of two; love further extended is adultery, not matrimony.

26. Nevertheless Spiritual love polluteth not a virgin; *Beia* might therefore without crime (before her promise to *Gabritius*) have contracted spiritual love, to the end that she might thereby be made more cheerful, more pure, and fitter for the business of matrimony.

27. Procreation of children is the end of lawful Wedlock. Now that the Infant may be born more vigorous and gallant, let both the combatants be cleansed from every scab and spot, before they both go up to their marriage bed, and let nothing unnecessary cleave unto them, because from pure seed comes a purified generation, and so the chaste wedlock of *Sol* and *Luna* shall be finished when they shall enter into love bed-chamber, and be conjoined, and she shall receive a soul from her husband by embracing him; from this copulation a most potent King shall arise, whose father will be *Sol* and his mother *Luna*.

Note:

†. Reprinted from the *Arcanum, or Great Secret of Hermetic Philosophy*, and published in *Fasciculus Chemicus, or Chymical Collections*. Translated by James Hasolle [Elias Ashmole], 1650. The Text has been modernized to match Westcott's translation. Westcott donated a copy of his edition of the *Hermetic Arcanum* to the Golden Dawn Library. A reader of the copy in the G.D. Library had written in the book the missing Lunar working from Ashmole's 1650 edition, and Gilbert feels that reader was W.B. Yeats. R.A. Gilbert wrote that "Ayton's real love, even within the Golden Dawn, had been alchemy, and it was from among his papers that I acquired my one link with Yeats. ... This was a G.D. Library copy of Westcott's translation of the anonymous *Hermetic Arcanum* (1893), which Yeats is known to have read and used at the Order's headquarters in Clipstone Street." See Gilbert's "The Quest of the Golden Dawn: A Cautionary Tale," in *Cauda Pavonis*, Vol. 8, No. 1, (Spring 1989), pp. 5-6.–D.K.

# Collectanea Hermetica

VOLUME I.

## The Hermetic Arcanum of Jean d'Espagnet

Preface and Notes by S. A.

*Price 2s. 6d. net.*

VOLUME II.

## The Divine Pymander of Hermes

*Price 3s. net.*

VOLUME III.

(*In preparation*)

## A Short Enquiry concerning the Hermetic Art. 1714, Anon.

Introduction and Notes by S. S. D. D.

*Price 2s. 6d. net.*

THEOSOPHICAL PUBLISHING SOCIETY
7, DUKE STREET, ADELPHI, LONDON, W.C.

Advertisement for the "Collectanea Hermetica"
Theosophical Publishing Society, (1894).

## *Collectanea Hermetica.*

Hermetic Arcanum of Penes Nos Unda Tagi. 1623. This is Vol. I of a series of tracts entitled "Colletanea Hermetica," edited by W. Wynn Westcott, M. B., D. P. H. (Supreme Magus of Rosicruciation Society, and Master of the Quatuor Coronati Lodge.) This vol. contains preface and notes by "Sapere Aude," Fra. R.R. et A.C. This is the Secret work of the Hermetic Philosophy wherein the Secrets of Nature and Art concerning the matter of the Philosopher's Stone and the manner of working are explained in an authentic and orderly manner. It is the work of an anonymous author, "Penes Nos Unda Tagi." 12mo, cloth, 56 pp.

Divine Pymander of Hermes Trismegistus. This work is Vol. II of the series of tracts entitled "Collectanea Hermetica," with a preface by the editor. This volume contains the English translation of Dr. Everard, 1650, of 17 tracts of which the "Pymander" is one, attributed to Hermes Trismegistus, otherwise Mercurius Termaximus, or in the Egyptian language, Thoth, or Taautes,, or Tat. 12mo, cloth, 117 pp.

Vol. III will be published in due time, which title is to be "A Short Enquiry concerning the Hermetic Art"; 1714. Anon. Introduction and notes by S. S., D. D. Vol. IV, to entitled "The Dream of Scipio," with notes by L. O. "The Golden Verses of Pythagoras," prepared by A. E. A. Prices, Vol. I, two shillings and six pence; Vol. II, three shillings; Vol. III, two shillings and six pence; Vol. IV, price not yet fixed. Published by Theosophical Publishing Society, 7 Duke Street, Adelphi, W. C.. London, Eng.

Advertisement for the "Collectanea Hermetica"
*Miscellaneous Notes and Queries.* Vol. XII, No. 6, June (1894).

# BIBLIOGRAPHY.

ENCHIRIDION PHYSICÆ RESTITUTÆ, In quo verus Naturæ concentus exponitur, plurimíque antiquæ Philosophiæ errores per canones & certas demonstrationes dilucidè aperiuntur. *Tractatus alter inscriptus* ARCANUM HERMETICÆ PHILOSOPHIÆ OPUS: in quo occulta Naturæ & Artis circa lapidis Philosophorum materiam & operandi modum canonice & ordinatè fiunt manifesta. *Utrumque opus ejusdem authoris anonymi.* SPES MEA EST IN AGNO. PARIS, Apud NICOLAVM BVON, sub signo D. Claudij, & Hominis Syluestris, 1623.

ENCHIRIDION PHYSICÆ RESTITUTÆ, In quo verus Naturæ concentus exponitur, plurimíque antiquæ Philosophiæ errores per canones & certas demonstrationes dilucidè aperiuntur. *Tractatus alter inscriptus* ARCANUM HERMETICÆ PHILOSOPHIÆ OPUS: in quo occulta Naturæ & Artis circa lapidis Philosophorum materiam & operandi modum canonice & ordinatè fiunt manifesta. *Utrumque opus ejusdem authoris anonymi.* SPES MEA EST IN AGNO. 3rd edition. Paris: N. de Sercy, 1642. [The Ashmole 1650 edition was based on this version.]

ENCHIRIDION PHYSICÆ RESTITUTÆ, In quo verus Naturæ concentus exponitur, plurimíque antiquæ Philosophiæ errores per canones & certas demonstrationes dilucidè aperiuntur. *Tractatus alter inscriptus* ARCANUM HERMETICÆ PHILOSOPHIÆ OPUS: in quo occulta Naturæ & Artis circa lapidis Philosophorum materiam & operandi modum canonice & ordinatè fiunt manifesta. *Utrumque opus ejusdem authoris anonymi.* SPES MEA EST IN AGNO. 4th edition. emendata & aucta. Rothomagi, 1647.

Dee, Arthur. *Fasciculus Chemicus; or, Chymical collections, Expressing the Ingress, Progress, and Egress, of the Secret Hermetick Science, out of the choisest and most famous authors. Collected and digested in such an order, that it may prove to the advantage, not only of the Beginners, but Proficients of this high Art, by none hitherto disposed in this Method. Whereunto is added, The Arcanum; or, Grand secret of Hermetick Philosophy.* Both made English by John Hasolle [Elias Ashmole], Esquire, Qui est Mercuriophilus Anglicus. Printed by J. Flesher for Richard Mynne, at the sign of St. Paul in Little Britian, 1650.

ENCHIRIDION PHYSICÆ RESTITUTÆ; *or, The Summary of Physicks Recovered. Wherein the true Harmony of Nature is explained, and many Errours of the Ancient Philosophers, by Canons and certain Deomnstrations are clearly evidence and evinced.* Translated by John Everard. Printed by W. Bentley. London, 1651.

Collectanea Hermetica Vol. I: An English Translation of the HERMETIC ARCANUM OF PENES NOS UNDA TAGI [Jean D'Espagnet]. 1623. With a Preface and Notes by "SAPERE AUDE", Fra. R.R. et A.C. Edited by W. Wynn Westcott, M.B. D.P.H. Theosophical Publishing Society, 1893.

*Jean D'Espagnet's the summary of physics restored: the 1651 translation with D'Espagnet's Arcanum (1650).* Edited by Thomas Willard. (English Renaissance Hermeticism). New York: Garland Publishing, 1999.

# NOTES

ON THE

# "CONTRIBUTORS."

---

Robert Allen Bartlett is a practicing alchemist, professional chemist, and author. In 1974, he pursued an intensive course of alchemical study at the Paracelsus Research Society (later Paracelsus College) under the guidance of Frater Albertus. In 1979, he received his B.S. Degree in Chemistry and immediately began work at Paracelsus Laboratories as the Chief Chemist. Robert currently lives in the Pacific Northwest where he has taught classes and workshops on practical alchemy since 2002. He is an instructor with the Spagyric Institute of Alchemy and the International Alchemy Guild's online alchemy school. He has presented the Spagyrics Workshop at the International Alchemy Conference along with being a keynote speaker. His books, *Real Alchemy, A Primer of Practical Alchemy* and *The Way of the Crucible* are available through Ibis Press. His website is: www.RealAlchemy.org.

Robert A. Gilbert has written extensively on Western Esotericism, particularly on occultism and esoteric Freemasonry during the Victorian era. He is the author of a long series of works on the Hermetic Order of the Golden Dawn and its major personalities, including both a biography and bibliography of A.E. Waite, and the definitive edition of *The House of the Hidden Light*, a joint work of Waite and Arthur Machen. He is currently writing on aspects of mysticism and of early Gnosticism. Dr. Gilbert read Philosophy and Psychology at the University of Bristol and received his doctorate from the University of London. He is also the editor of *The Christian Parapsychologist*.

DARCY KÜNTZ is the director of the Golden Dawn Research Trust which was founded in 1998. The Research Trust is preserving the teachings, ritual, history, practices, documents, letters, and books of the Hermetic Order of the Golden Dawn (as it existed between the dates 1887-1930). We are preserving this material so that the information may be available and remain accessible to scholars now and in the future. Some of his published work includes: *Complete Golden Dawn Cipher Manuscript* (1996); *Golden Dawn Sourcebook* (1996); *The Historic Structure of the Original Golden Dawn Temples* (1999); *The Golden Dawn American Source Book* (2000); *Sent From the Second Order* (2005); *Ancient Texts of the Golden Rosicrucians* (2008).

WILLIAM WYNN WESTCOTT was one of the founders of the Order of the Golden Dawn. In the Order he used the motto V.H. Frater "Sapere Aude", which translates as "Dare to be wise". Westcott was involved in a number of Orders some of which are the Societas Rosicruciana In Anglia, Freemasonry, and the Coronati Lodge #2076, the premier Lodge of Masonic Research. Westcott wrote many medical and therapeutic works, but he is better known by his Masonic and Rosicrucian works, among them are: *The Sepher Yetzirah*; *The Isiac Tablet of Cardinal Bembo*; *An Essay on Alchemy*; *Numbers, Their Occult Power and Mystic Virtues*; *The Hieroglyphic Figures of Nicholas Flamel*, and numerous volumes of the *Collectanea Hermetica*.

CPSIA information can be obtained at www.ICGtesting.com
231734LV00001B/2/P
9 781926 982007